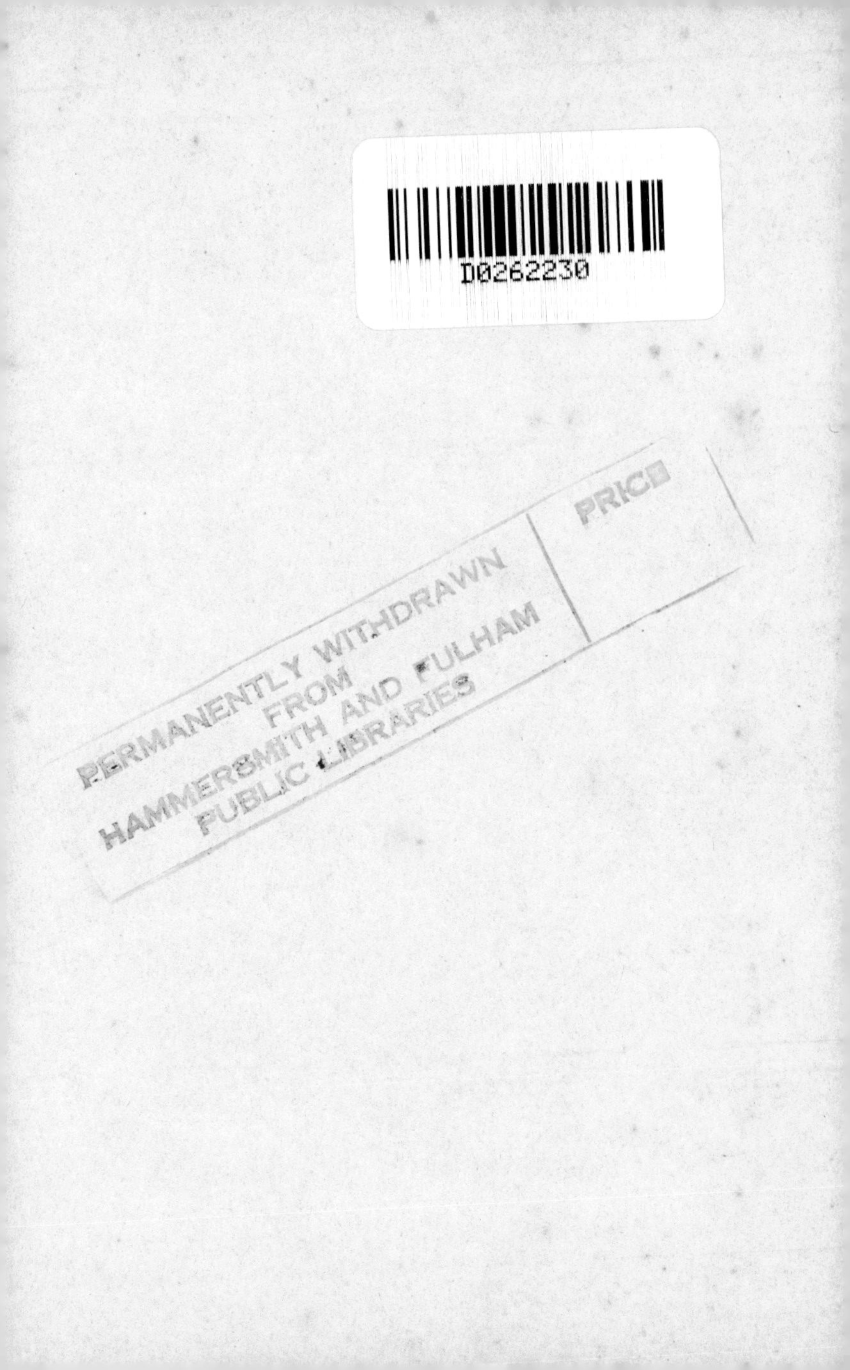

Enid Blyton's
BRER RABBIT AGAIN

First published 1963
This reprint 1987

Published by Dean, an imprint of
The Hamlyn Publishing Group Limited,
Bridge House, 69 London Road, Twickenham,
Middlesex TW1 3SB, England

ISBN 0 603 03254 0

Printed and bound by Purnell Book Production Ltd.,
Paulton, Bristol.
Member of BPCC plc

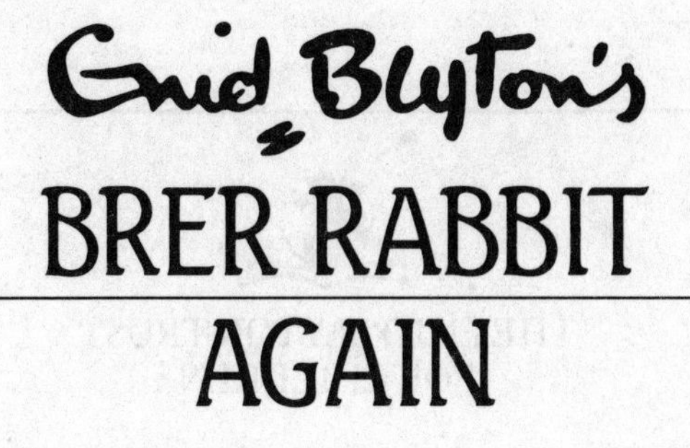
Enid Blyton's
BRER RABBIT
AGAIN

DEAN

THE ENID BLYTON TRUST FOR CHILDREN

We hope you will enjoy this book. Please think for a moment about those children who are too ill to do the exciting things you and your friends do.

Help them by sending a donation, large or small, to THE ENID BLYTON TRUST FOR CHILDREN. The Trust will use all your gifts to help children who are sick or handicapped and need to be made happy and comfortable.

Please send your postal order or cheque to:
The Enid Blyton Trust for Children,
International House,
1 St Katharine's Way,
London, E1 9UN

Thank you very much for your help.

CONTENTS

Brer Rabbit and the Glue

Once Brer Rabbit had a job to do in his garden. Some little bits of his fence had broken, and he guessed he would stick them back with glue.

So he put the glue-pot on the fire, stirred it up, and when it had melted he took it into the garden. He gathered together the bits of wood that wanted sticking, and began.

He was so busy that he didn't notice Brer Fox coming up behind him. It was only when Brer Fox pounced on him that he knew Brer Fox was there.

"Got you!" cried Brer Fox.

"Now, Brer Fox, please let me go," said Brer Rabbit in a calm sort of voice. "Can't you see I'm very busy?"

"What's that matter?" said Brer Fox, still holding tightly to Brer Rabbit. "I shall be busy soon too—having you for my dinner!"

"Oh, Brer Fox, don't be mean," said Brer Rabbit. "Just let me finish this job, for goodness' sake! I promised I would do it to-day, and I always like to keep my promises."

"What are you doing?" asked Brer Fox, gazing round at the glue-brushes, the glue-pot, and the wood.

"I'm mending this fence with glue," said Brer Rabbit. "Now don't ask if you can help, Brer Fox, because you couldn't. It's too tricky a job for you."

"What do you mean—too tricky for me?" said Brer Fox crossly. "You're not trying to make out that you are cleverer than I am, are you?"

"Oh no, not at all," said Brer Rabbit, dipping his brush in the glue. "It's only that I think you would make a mess of it."

Brer Fox glared at Brer Rabbit, who was now peacefully painting a board with strong glue. "Look here, Brer Rabbit," he began.

"Can't. I'm busy," answered Brer Rabbit. "Let me finish this job and I'll come with you, Brer Fox. But for goodness' sake don't interfere. I don't want everything spoilt."

Of course that made Brer Fox snatch up a big glue-brush and start work at once. "Hoo! I'll show you that I can glue things just as well as you can," he growled.

Brer Rabbit noticed that Brer Fox's tail was brushing against the garden-gate behind them. He grinned to himself. He put down his glue-brush and picked up the piece of wood he was working on to see if it was nicely done. When he set to work again, he didn't pick up his glue-brush—no, he took Brer Fox's tail, and dipped that into the glue-pot instead!

Brer Fox was angry. "Hey, you cuckoo! That's my tail!"

"Sorry," said Brer Rabbit. "It's so like a brush, Brer Fox. Sorry, sorry, sorry!"

Brer Fox took his tail out of the glue-pot and arranged it behind him again. It touched the gate as before. And pretty soon it stuck hard to the gate. Brer Rabbit watched out of the corner of his eye and grinned away to himself.

"I'll just go and get some more glue," he said to Brer Fox after a while, and he got up. Brer Fox got up to go with him, for he wasn't going to let Brer Rabbit go out of his sight, now that he had caught him so neatly. But something held him by the tail.

Brer Fox swung round angrily—and saw that his tail was stuck fast to the gate. "My tail's stuck!" he cried. "Brer Rabbit, you did it on purpose! Unstick it at once."

"What—and let you pounce on me again!" grinned Brer Rabbit. "I'm not such a silly as you think, Brer Fox. You can stay there all day, if you like."

"I shall *not*!" yelled Brer Fox, and he tugged at his tail. Then he groaned deeply, for it hurt him very much. He sat and scowled at Brer Rabbit, who stood just out of reach, swinging the glue-pot.

"I'll get you a pair of scissors and you can cut your tail off," said Brer Rabbit kindly.

"Don't be silly," said Brer Fox, groaning again.

"There's no pleasing you," said Brer Rabbit. "So good-bye I'll be back again soon to see how your tail is getting on."

Brer Rabbit went indoors, and watched from the window. He knew Brer Wolf was coming along that way soon—and sure enough he soon came ambling by. He pushed open Brer Rabbit's gate to see if Brer Rabbit was anywhere about, and he nearly knocked over Brer Fox, who was just the other side of it, his tail still stuck tightly to the gate.

"Hie! Be careful!" yelled Brer Fox.

"Heyo, Brer Fox," said Brer Wolf in surprise. "What are you doing here?"

"I'm stuck," said Brer Fox.

"Stuck? What do you mean, 'stuck'?" said Brer Wolf in still greater surprise.

"Don't you know what 'stuck' means?" said Brer Fox snappily. "My tail's stuck to the gate. That tiresome Brer Rabbit did it. Now he's offered me a pair of scissors to cut off my tail."

"Well, that's what you'll have to do, isn't it?" said Brer Wolf, looking at the stuck-fast tail. "You'll have to stay here all night and day if you don't."

"Now do you think I'm going to cut off my beautiful tail?" demanded Brer Fox. "You must be mad!"

"Well, what else is there to do?" said Brer Wolf.

"I don't know," said Brer Fox sulkily.

"Ah—*I* know!" cried Brer Wolf. "I can take the gate off! Then you can go home, carrying the gate, can't you?"

"Well—it sounds silly, but perhaps it's the best thing to do," said Brer Fox gloomily. "Brer Rabbit will lose his gate then—and serve him right!"

Brer Wolf heaved at the gate till it came off its hinges. Then Brer Fox took it on his back, with his tail still tightly stuck to it, and walked slowly off home, groaning all the way because of the weight of the gate and the pain in his tail.

When he got home he asked Brer Wolf to get a great bath of hot water. When it was ready, Brer Fox sat beside it, with his tail and the gate in the water, hoping to soak off the glue.

It came off after twelve hours' soaking, and poor Brer Fox got such a cold in his tail that he had to wear a handkerchief round it for three days to keep his tail from sneezing itself off.

He chopped up Brer Rabbit's gate and burnt it, and the next day found to his great rage that his own gate was gone—and there it was swinging gaily in Brer Rabbit's gateway.

"You just wait, Brer Rabbit, you just wait," he yelled.

"Righto!" yelled back Brer Rabbit. "I don't know what you want me to wait for, Brer Fox, but I'll certainly wait. Oh yes, I'll wait all right!"

So he's waiting—and Brer Fox's gate is still swinging merrily in Brer Rabbit's front garden. It *is* so annoying for Brer Fox!

Brer Rabbit Plays a Trick !

Now one morning Brer Fox went fishing and he caught a fine lot of fish. He was mighty pleased with himself and he went along through the trees, whistling a merry tune.

Brer Rabbit heard him and peeped round a tree. When he saw the fish, he rubbed his hands. Just what he wanted for his dinner.

He danced out from behind the tree and called to Brer Fox, " Heyo, Brer Fox ! That's a mighty fine lot of fish you've got there ! "

" Yes," said Brer Fox. " And there's none for you, Brer Rabbit—so just go home."

" Oh, let me walk with you a little way ! " said Brer Rabbit, sidling up near the fish. Brer Fox put them over his other shoulder.

" If you come any nearer I'll grab you, Brer Rabbit," he said. " I'd like fish for dinner, and rabbit-pie for supper."

But Brer Rabbit got so near that his nose almost touched the fish, and Brer Fox guessed he was thinking out a trick to get some for himself. So he turned round on Brer Rabbit, flashed out his paw and caught hold of his shoulder. Then Brer Rabbit was nearly caught ! He wriggled away and set off at top speed, with Brer Fox on his tail. My, that was a chase ! In and out of the trees they went, with Brer Fox grabbing all the time. Brer Rabbit couldn't see a hole anywhere to get into, and at last, when Brer Fox had almost got him by the bobtail, he raced up a tree, and sat there in the branches.

Now Brer Fox wasn't much good at climbing trees, and he felt pretty certain that Brer Rabbit would push him down if he did get up, so he sat down at the foot, panting and puffing, his string of fish beside him.

"You stay up there, Brer Rabbit!" said Brer Fox. "You stay up there! You'll be mighty hungry by night-time—but when you come down, you'll be caught. Yes, you'll be caught."

Brer Rabbit said nothing. He just sat and grinned to himself. He knew a thing or two about that tree. He got back his breath, and he grinned all the time.

Brer Fox ate one of his fish. Brer Rabbit heard him cracking the backbone, and he looked down. The string of fish was stretched out beside Brer Fox—it looked good, and Brer Rabbit was hungry.

Now a good way up the trunk of the tree there was a hole where the squirrels used to live. Brer Rabbit knew it well. He knew that it led right down into the bottom of the tree, and he knew, too, that there was a burrow there that led beneath the tree and up again under the big bramble bush not far from Brer Fox.

So down he went into the hole, dropped quietly to the

bottom, scampered down the burrow, and came up not far from Brer Fox. He cut himself a prickly bramble spray, carefully pushed it along the ground, and hooked a fish off the string. He pulled it back towards him, whilst Brer Fox went on munching his meal, gazing up into the trees.

Then down the burrow went Brer Rabbit and up into the tree again. He sat on a branch just above Brer Fox and began to eat the fish. He dropped the bones down on to Brer Fox.

Brer Fox felt the bones and looked to see what they were. He thought that Brer Rabbit was throwing bits of twig down on him, but when he saw that they were fish-bones, he jumped up with a yell.

And he saw old Brer Rabbit sitting up in the tree as large as life, munching away at one of his fish.

" Brer Rabbit ! Where did you get that fish from ? " yelled Brer Fox. " It's mine ! "

" Oh, Brer Fox, how can you say that ? " said Brer Rabbit. " I couldn't have reached down and got it, could I, with you sitting there ? "

Brer Fox was mighty angry and mighty puzzled. He glared at Brer Rabbit, pulled his string of fish closer to him, and sat down again, trying to puzzle out how Brer Rabbit could have got the fish.

Well, it wasn't long before old Brer Rabbit played the same trick on him again, and once more Brer Fox felt a shower of bones on his head, and counted his string of fish, to find another missing !

He stared up at Brer Rabbit in the greatest astonishment. How *could* Brer Rabbit have reached down the tall trunk and got a fish again ?

" Grin all you like, Brer Rabbit," said Brer Fox, " but I'm not going to let you get another fish. I'm going to stand here and look up into this tree all the time, then there'll be no slipping down the trunk and reaching out for a fish. And what's more, I'm going to hang the fish on that bramble bush over there, right away from the tree!"

So he threw the string of fish over the bramble bush and then he stood looking up into the tree, meaning to make quite sure that Brer Rabbit didn't come down and steal any more fish.

Brer Rabbit stared back at Brer Fox. "Don't look at me like that, Brer Fox," he begged. "I just can't bear it."

"Well, go higher up then!" grinned Brer Fox. "The higher you go, the better it suits me!"

So Brer Rabbit leapt up higher, and the leaves closed around him so that Brer Fox couldn't see him. But all the same, Brer Fox still stood there, looking hard up the tree to make sure that old Brer Rabbit didn't come down.

But Brer Rabbit slipped quietly into the hollow trunk again, down the burrow, and up under the bramble bush. He took the string of fish, hung them over his shoulder, and skipped off home with them, while Brer Fox still went on looking and looking up the tree.

Pretty soon Brer Fox felt hungry again and thought he would like another of his fish. So he turned round to get one—and the whole string was gone!

Brer Fox gave a yell and looked all round the wood. Not a creature was to be seen except a little Jack Sparrow up in a tree.

"Hey!" shouted Brer Fox to the sparrow. "Have you seen my fish?"

"Yes," said the Jack Sparrow. "I saw Brer Rabbit with them. You go after him, Brer Fox."

"He's up this tree," said Brer Fox angrily. "You're just saying that because you're a friend of his, and you guess I'll go off through the woods and let Brer Rabbit come down and escape. Well, I won't! I'll catch him when he comes down, and then I'll go hunting for the thief."

Well, old Brer Fox, he waited and he waited for Brer Rabbit to come down that tree, but he didn't. How could he, when he was sitting at home eating fish-pie? Brer Fox sat there all that night, but when morning came he was so stiff and hungry that he had to go home.

On the way he passed Brer Rabbit's house and saw Mrs. Rabbit getting the breakfast. There was such a nice smell that Brer Fox stopped and sniffed.

"What are you having for breakfast, Mrs. Rabbit?" he called.

But it wasn't Mrs. Rabbit who answered. It was old Brer Rabbit himself! He poked his cheeky head out of the window and shouted to Brer Fox:

"We're having fish-cakes, Brer Fox, that's what we're having—and mighty good fish it is too! My, Brer Fox, where have you been all night? You do look tired and ill!"

Then Brer Fox knew he had been tricked again, and he looked so fierce that Brer Rabbit slammed down the window and bolted the door.

You be careful, Brer Rabbit! Brer Fox will think out a trick that will catch *you*, one of these days!

Brer Wolf Gets a Surprise

ONCE, WHEN Brer Rabbit was gambolling through the wood, singing a silly little song that he had made up himself, he heard a curious noise.

He stopped his song and listened. He didn't hear the noise again, so he went on singing:

Oh, if I were a little bee,
Humming round a jim-jam tree,
It would be curious to see
Growing on the end of me
Not a tail or anything
Except a most unpleasant sting!
Zz, zz, zz, zz . . .

Brer Rabbit stopped his song suddenly again, because he had heard the peculiar noise. He stood and listened, and didn't sing again. The noise seemed to come from a tree nearby.

Brer Rabbit looked up into the tree. Nothing there. He walked all round the tree and back again. Nothing there!

But still the noise went on, "Hissssss! Spit! Hissssss! Yee-ow, ee-ow! Hissssssssss!"

"Funny!" said Brer Rabbit, staring up into the tree again. "Nobody there—and yet it sounds like a houseful of cats in a temper!"

Brer Rabbit climbed up the tree a little way—and then he came to a hole. He peered down into the hole. At once a great noise came from the hole that startled Brer Rabbit so much he nearly fell down the tree.

"Baby wild-cats!" said Brer Rabbit. "Yes, that's what's making all the noise. Poor little things—their mother has gone off and left them. I guess I'd better take them home with me and give them some milk."

Brer Rabbit fetched his bag, which he had left on the ground. Then he took out his silk handkerchief and let it down into the hole. One of the kittens hissed and spat at it, and then dug its claws into the silk. Brer Rabbit quickly lifted up his handkerchief, kitten and all! He dropped the kitten into the bag, shook the hanky free from its claws, and put it down to catch the next kitten. Up it came, clawing at the handkerchief, and was dropped into the bag.

There were five kittens altogether, all as wild and fierce as each other. What a noise they made! How they fought inside the bag! How they yowled and scratched at one another! Really, it was terrible to hear them.

"Fight all you like!" said Brer Rabbit, putting the bag over his shoulders. "I know it's what you wild kittens like better than anything! Fight all you like!"

Now as he went along home, with his bag of kittens on his shoulder, who should come pounding along through the wood

but old Brer Wolf, looking mighty hungry and mighty fierce. He saw Brer Rabbit and pounced on him before Brer Rabbit could slip round the trees.

"Ha!" said Brer Wolf, and his whiskers shot up and down. "Ha! So you're home from market, are you, with your bag full of goodies. Well, you just hand it over to *me*!"

"Let me go, Brer Wolf," said Brer Rabbit, wriggling. "Your claws are sharp. And don't you be silly enough to take my bag either!"

"What's in the bag?" asked Brer Wolf, sniffing.

"A litter of wild kittens," said Brer Rabbit. "And my, they're wild, I can tell you!"

Brer Wolf laughed loudly. "Do you suppose I'm going to believe that you are carrying a bag of wild kittens about with you, Brer Rabbit?" he asked. "No—I guess that bag's full of good meat!"

The kittens had all become perfectly quiet when they heard Brer Wolf's voice, for they were afraid of him. So they didn't say a word. They just lay as quiet as could be in the bag.

"You give that bag to me, Brer Rabbit," said Brer Wolf. "If you don't, I'll take it—and you too!"

Now just at that moment Brer Rabbit caught sight of two bright green eyes gleaming through the trees—and he saw that it was the mother wild-cat! She hadn't really left her kittens—she had just gone to get a drink of water from the stream for herself. When she had gone back she had found her tree-hole empty, and she had flown into a tremendous rage.

She called her mate, and he called five other wild-cats. " We will go to find the stolen kittens ! " hissed Cousin Wild-cat. " Follow me ! "

And that was how it was that Brer Rabbit suddenly saw the fierce and angry eyes of the mother wild-cat, and, behind her, six more pairs of green eyes too ! He began to shiver and shake, for an army of wild-cats is the fiercest thing in the world !

" All right," he said to Brer Wolf. " You take my bag of meat. Here you are, you're welcome to it ! "

He pushed his bag into Brer Wolf's arms and then slipped behind a tree. Brer Wolf was pleased.

" Ho ! " he shouted after Brer Rabbit. " You're a little coward, you are ! You'd run away from anything ! "

He opened the bag, meaning to eat the meat at once —and out sprang five wild kittens, all their claws out, spitting and hissing and snarling like a hundred fire works going off together !

Brer Wolf got a dreadful shock—but an even bigger one was waiting for him.

As soon as the seven wild-cats saw their kittens jumping out of the bag, they gave a snarl and leapt on poor, scared Brer Wolf!

My word, they were like a swarm of big bees all over him! He shook them off and they came again. Their claws dug into him like hundreds of pins and needles, and they spat and hissed like kettles on the boil!

"We'll teach you to take our kittens!" snarled Cousin Wild-cat. "We'll teach you. Hissssssss!"

Brer Wolf shook the cats off his big brown hairy body and ran for his life. The wild-cats picked up the delighted kittens and ran back to the hollow tree with them, meowling in joy.

Brer Rabbit popped his head out of a hole as Brer Wolf rushed by, scratched and torn.

"Hallo, Brer Wolf!" he cried. "My, how dreadful you look! Have you been shot out of a gun or something?"

"Now look here, Brer Rabbit, if I'd known that bag was full of wild kittens, I'd have run a mile!" said Brer Wolf angrily.

"What a little coward you are, Brer Wolf!" said Brer Rabbit. "You'd run away from anything! I *told* you the bag was full of kittens!"

"Grrrrrrrrrr!" said Brer Wolf, and tore home to bandage all his scratches. He did look a funny sight when he had finished!

Brer Bear's Bad Memory

BRER BEAR always had a bad memory. He forgot things a hundred times a week, and sometimes it was very awkward.

One day he invited Brer Wolf and Brer Fox to tea the next day—but he had forgotten the invitation when the time came, and he went off to pay a call on his old aunt. So when Brer Fox and Brer Wolf turned up, expecting a most delicious tea, they found Brer Bear's house shut and nobody in at all.

They were angry with Brer Bear, and he was most upset. He sat in his front garden looking very miserable that evening when Brer Rabbit happened along.

"What's up, Brer Bear?" asked Brer Rabbit. So Brer Bear told him.

"If only I could think of something that would remind me to remember things," said Brer Bear.

"Well, why don't you tie a knot in your handkerchief every time you want to remember something?" asked Brer Rabbit. He took out his own yellow handkerchief and showed it to Brer Bear. It had a knot in it. "Look," said Brer Rabbit, pointing to the knot. "That's to remind me to buy some fresh carrots on my way home."

"What a very, very good idea!" said Brer Bear, delighted. "I'll do the same! You just come along to-morrow, Brer Rabbit, and you'll see how well I am remembering everything!"

So the next morning Brer Rabbit ambled along, and there was Brer Bear in his house, looking at a knot in his handkerchief with a very long face.

" Brer Rabbit, this knot business is not going to work," he said dolefully. " Now I can't remember what I put the knot there for ! "

Brer Rabbit put up his hand and hid a grin. " Why, Brer Bear," he said, " *I* can tell you ! You kindly asked me to dinner to-day ! "

Brer Bear looked surprised—and well he might, for he certainly hadn't asked Brer Rabbit to dinner. But as his memory was so bad he thought Brer Rabbit was right, and he set to work to prepare a tasty dinner.

Brer Rabbit enjoyed it very much. He thanked Brer Bear and went skipping home, grinning to think how Brer Bear was so easily tricked !

The next day along went Brer Rabbit again—and once more Brer Bear was looking at his handkerchief in dismay, wondering what he had tied the knot there for.

" I simply can't remember, Brer Rabbit ! " he said. " Now what *did* I tie that knot there for ? "

" To remind you to give me one of your jars of new honey ! " said Brer Rabbit at once. Brer Bear stared at him in surprise and scratched his head. But no amount of scratching could make him remember that he had promised Brer Rabbit some honey. Still, he liked to keep his promises, so he got down a jar and gave it to Brer Rabbit.

" All the same," said Brer Bear, " I'm *not* going to tie knots in my handkerchief any more, Brer Rabbit. It's just no use at all."

Well, Brer Bear untied the knot, and that night, although he wanted to remember quite a lot of things the next day, he didn't tie any knots in his hanky at all. He just put it on the window-sill and left it there.

Now Brer Rabbit hopped along that night and spied the handkerchief on the sill. He took it up and put two knots in it. Then he grinned and hopped off.

When he came along the next day he found poor Brer Bear in a great way, with the handkerchief on the table in front of him.

" Oh, Brer Rabbit ! " said Brer Bear, " this is worse than ever ! I don't even *remember* putting knots in my handkerchief —as well as not remembering what I tied them for ! "

" Dear, dear ! " spoke up Brer Rabbit, with a grin. " It's a good thing I'm always able to help you, Brer Bear. You put *that* knot in to remind you to shake your fist at Brer Wolf when he comes by—and you put *that* one in to remind you to buy some lettuces from me this morning."

" Did I really ? " said Brer Bear, astonished. " Brer Rabbit, my memory is getting worse each day ! "

" Well, here are the lettuces you said you wanted," said Brer Rabbit, putting three down on the table. " Sixpence, please, Brer Bear."

Brer Bear paid out sixpence and looked at the lettuces in a puzzled way. He didn't like lettuces. Then why did he say he would buy some ? He couldn't make it out.

" Look, here comes Brer Wolf ! " said Brer Rabbit. " That's the second knot in your hanky, Brer Bear. Shake your fist at him ! "

So poor Brer Bear went to the window and shook his fist at Brer Wolf when he went by. Brer Wolf was most amazed, and could hardly believe his eyes. But he was in a hurry, so he didn't say anything about it.

Again that night Brer Rabbit slipped along and put a knot into Brer Bear's hanky. In the morning he arrived at Brer Bear's as usual, and saw the knotted handkerchief sticking out of Brer Bear's pocket.

"Heyo, Brer Bear!" he cried. "Have you remembered what that knot is for this time?"

"Just take a look at this, Brer Rabbit," said Brer Bear, in an angry voice, and he stuck a piece of paper under Brer Rabbit's nose. On it was written in large letters:

"I HAVE NOT PUT ANY KNOTS IN MY HANKY TO-NIGHT.
"(Signed) BRER BEAR."

"Do you see that?" said Brer Bear. "Well, I wrote that last night before I went off to sleep, Brer Rabbit. And yet there's a knot in my hanky this morning. I think perhaps *you* know something about that, don't you?"

Brer Rabbit grinned. "Well, maybe I can tell you what it's there for," he said.

"Yes—you'll tell me I asked you to tea, or something like that!" said Brer Bear. "But, Brer Rabbit, I know better this time—that knot's there to remind me to shake you till your teeth rattle in your head! Yes—that's what that knot is there for!"

But Brer Rabbit didn't wait for Brer Bear to obey the knot! He scampered off, lippitty-clippitty, laughing to think how he had tricked poor old Brer Bear.

As for Brer Bear, he never tied another knot in his handkerchief, and he kept such a close watch for Brer Rabbit that that scamp didn't dare to go near him for weeks and weeks!

Brer Rabbit is So Cunning

Once, when Brer Rabbit was trotting along over a field, the wind blew some dead leaves out of the ditch into his face. Brer Rabbit got a real fright, and he tore off as if a hundred dogs were after him!

Well, it happened that Brer Fox and Brer Bear saw him running away, and they laughed to think that a few leaves had frightened Brer Rabbit. They went about among all the animals, telling them what a coward Brer Rabbit was, and how he had run away because of a few leaves.

When people met Brer Rabbit after that, they grinned slyly, and asked him whether he had had any more frights, and Brer Rabbit got very tired of it.

"I'm as brave as any of you!" he said. "And braver too!"

"Well, show us what a brave man you are, then!" cried every one, and they giggled at Brer Rabbit's angry face.

Brer Rabbit went off in a temper, and he thought and thought how he might show every one that he was a brave fellow. Then he grinned and slapped his knee.

"I'll soon show them!" he chuckled. "My, they'll get a fright, but it will serve them right!"

Then Brer Rabbit went to work out his idea. He took seven of his tin plates, made a hole in the middle of each, and threaded them together on a thick string. My, what a noise they made when he shook the string!

Then he took a big piece of glass from his cucumber-frame and ran his wet paw up and down it to see if it would make a good noise. It did! Oh, what a squeaking, squealing noise it made! Brer Rabbit grinned to himself.

Well, that night Brer Rabbit took the string of tin plates and the piece of glass with him, and climbed up a tree not far from Brer Fox's house. When he was comfortably settled, he began to enjoy himself.

He moaned and howled like twenty cats. He yelped like a dozen dogs. He screeched like a hundred parrots. "Oh-ee-oo-ee, ie-oh-ee-oh, YOW, YOW, YOW!"

Then he shook the string hard that joined the tin plates together, and they all jangled through the quiet night as if a thousand dustbins had gone mad and were dancing in a ring. "Clang, jang, clang, jang, clinky, clanky, clang, JANG!"

Brer Rabbit nearly fell out of the tree with laughing at the awful noise he made. Next, he took the big piece of glass, wetted his paw, and began to run it up and down the glass.

"EEEEEEEE-OOOO, EEEEEEEE-OOOOO!" it went, and all the wakened animals round about shivered and shook to hear such a dreadful squealing noise.

Then Brer Rabbit jangled his plates again. "Clang, jang, clang, jang, clinky, clanky, clang, jang!"

Brer Fox was sitting up in bed, as scared as could be. He couldn't for the life of him imagine what the noise was.

Brer Wolf was hiding under his bed. Brer Bear and Mrs. Bear were clinging together, crying on each other's shoulders, they were so frightened.

All the other animals were trembling, too, wondering what was going to happen next.

"Yow, YOW, YOW!" yelled Brer Rabbit. "Clinkity, clang, jang!" went his tin plates. "EeeeeeEEeeeeEEE-ooooo!" went his paw, squeaking up the glass.

At last Brer Rabbit hopped down his tree, ran to a tumble-down shed nearby, put all his things there, and then made his way to Brer Fox's house. He knocked loudly on the door, "BLIM, BLAM!"

Brer Fox got such a shock that he fell out of bed. "Who's there?" he said in a trembling voice.

"Me, Brer Rabbit," said Brer Rabbit. "I've come to see what all the noise is about."

"Oh, Brer Rabbit, dear Brer Rabbit, I'm so glad to see you," said Brer Fox, almost falling over himself to open the door. "Do come in. I've been scared out of my life. Whatever is that noise, do you think?"

"I don't know," said Brer Rabbit untruthfully. "Unless it is old Brer Elephant rampaging round, making a frightful noise. I just came along to see if you were all right, Brer Fox."

"Well, that's mighty kind of you, Brer Rabbit," said Brer Fox. "I wonder you're not afraid to be out, with all that

noise around. What are you going to do now? Don't leave me!"

"I'm just off to see if Brer Wolf and Brer Bear are all right," said Brer Rabbit. "Maybe they are scared and will be glad to see me."

Off he went, and found Brer Wolf and Brer Bear just as scared as Brer Fox. My, they thought he was a very brave fellow to be out that night!

"We'll look in the morning and see if we can see any signs of old Brer Elephant," said Brer Rabbit. "It's a wet, muddy night and maybe we'll find his footprints. Then we can follow them and see where he is!"

After Brer Rabbit had left his friends, he skipped and danced a bit with glee, and then he went to where he had hidden a big round log of wood, just the shape of an elephant's great foot. Brer Rabbit went all round about Brer Fox's house and Brer Bear's and Brer Wolf's, stamping the end of the big log into the mud, so that it looked for all the world as if a mighty big lot of feet had been going around there in the night.

Brer Rabbit giggled to himself when he had finished. He went back home to bed and slept well till the morning.

The next day he and all the other animals went to look for footprints. When the others saw the enormous marks in the mud they were as scared as could be.

"Those are elephant's footprints all right!" said Brer Fox. "I know elephant's marks when I see them. My, he was around here last night all right. I wonder he didn't knock my house down!"

"Let's follow the footprints," said Brer Rabbit.

"I don't think I want to do that," said Brer Bear, who didn't like the look of things at all.

"What! Are you afraid?" cried Brer Rabbit. "Well, *I'm* not! I'm going to see where these footmarks lead to, even if I have to go alone!"

Well, he followed the footprints in the mud, and they led him to the old tumbledown shed, as he knew they would, for he had put them there himself! Brer Fox and the others followed him at a good distance. Brer Rabbit tiptoed to the shed and looked inside.

He tiptoed back to the others at once. "Yes," said the cunning fellow, "he's in there all right! Fast asleep! I think I'll go and attack him whilst he's asleep!"

"What! Attack an elephant!" said Brer Wolf in the greatest astonishment. "Don't be silly."

"*I'm* not afraid of elephants!" said Brer Rabbit. "I'll just go in and bang him on the head! I guess he'll rush out in a mighty hurry, so be careful he doesn't knock you all over!"

"Come back, Brer Rabbit!" called Brer Fox, as Brer Rabbit tiptoed to the shed again. "You'll only make him angry, and he'll rush out and knock down all our houses!"

Brer Rabbit disappeared into the shed. He had a good laugh and then he began. He took up his string of tin plates and made them dance with a clanky-lanky clang-jang! He made his paw squeal up and down the glass. He yowled and howled. He took a tin trumpet from his pocket and blew hard, for he had once heard that elephants made a trumpeting sound.

Then he began to shout and yell in his own voice, "Take *that*, you great noisy creature! Take *that*, you stupid elephant! And that, and that, and that!"

Every time he said, "And *that!*" Brer Rabbit hit the side of the shed with a piece of wood and it made a terrible noise. Crash! Crash! Crash!

The animals waiting not far off shivered and shook. Brer Rabbit put his eye to a crack in the wall of the shed and grinned to see them.

Then he took a heap of paper bags out of his pocket, and blew them up one by one. He banged them with his hand and they went, Pop!

Pop! Pop! Pop! Pop! They sounded like guns shooting. Brer Rabbit jangled his plates again, and banged the shed with the piece of wood. You might have thought that at least twenty animals were fighting inside that shed!

And then Brer Rabbit took up the log that he had made the footprints with and sent it crashing through the other side of the shed, as if some big animal had fallen through it and was scrambling away. He began to shout.

"Run, Brer Elephant, run!" he yelled. "Run, or I'll get you! Run, run!"

Brer Fox, Brer Wolf, and all the others thought that the

elephant had crashed its way out of the shed and was loose. At once they fled to Brer Fox's house and bolted themselves in, trembling. Brer Rabbit saw them from the crack in the shed and laughed fit to kill himself.

When at last he stopped laughing he made his way to Brer Fox's house, panting as if he had been having a great fight. He knocked at the door, "blam, blam!"

"Who's there?" called Brer Fox, afraid.

"Brer Rabbit," said Brer Rabbit in a big voice. The door opened and all the animals came out. They crowded round Brer Rabbit, patted him on the back, hugged him and fussed him! My, it was grand for Brer Rabbit!

"You're a hero!" cried Brer Fox.

"The bravest creature in the world!" said Brer Bear.

"The strongest of us all!" said Brer Wolf.

"I'm glad you think so, friends," said Brer Rabbit. "There was a time when you called me a coward, and maybe if I remember which of you laughed at me then, I might treat them as I treated old Brer Elephant!"

"*We* wouldn't laugh at a brave man like Brer Rabbit!" shouted every one at once.

"Well, just see you don't!" said Brer Rabbit, and he put his nose in the air, threw out his chest, and walked off, looking mighty biggitty! And after that the animals were very careful to be polite to Brer Rabbit for a long, long time!

Brer Fox's Carrots

Now one year it happened that Brer Fox had a mighty good crop of carrots. They were very fine, and Brer Fox was so afraid that Brer Rabbit would be after them that he made himself a little shelter of bracken leaves and slept there each night to guard his field.

So whenever old Brer Rabbit came sniffing along that way there was Brer Fox, his sharp ears cocked, and his sharp nose sticking out of the bracken shelter.

" Well, well," said Brer Rabbit to himself. " If I don't get my share of those carrots in the field, I'll wait till they're pulled ! Maybe Brer Fox will hand me a few. He's got plenty."

So he watched and waited till he saw Brer Fox pulling his carrots. My, they were a fine juicy lot, and no mistake ! Brer Rabbit watched from the hedge, and he longed and longed for a taste of those carrots.

" Heyo, Brer Rabbit ! " said Brer Fox, with a grin. " *I* can seen you a-sitting there, with your nose woffling like a mouse's ! You can sit there all day if you like and watch the way I pull my carrots—but if you think you're going to nibble even the green tops of one, you'll have to think again ! "

" Why, Brer Fox, you've so many that surely you can spare one or two for an old friend like me," said Brer Rabbit.

" Old friend! Old *enemy*, you mean ! " said Brer Fox, with a snort. " Now, listen to me, Brer Rabbit—you can just make up your mind that these carrots belong to *me* ! And, what's more, I'm going to store them in my cellar and padlock the trap-door that leads to it ! And if you can get any carrots out of a locked-up cellar, why you're very welcome ! "

" Thanks, Brer Fox, thanks ! " said Brer Rabbit, seeming to be very grateful.

" Oh, you needn't thank me ! " said Brer Fox.

" But you said I was welcome to any carrots I could get out of your locked cellar," said Brer Rabbit. " And I was just thanking you for them."

" Then you're thanking me for nothing ! " said Brer Fox, pulling a great heap of carrots up at once. " For nothing is what you'll get, my fine friend ! "

Brer Rabbit grinned and disappeared. He ran off to Brer Fox's house, and sat in the garden and thought about that cellar. Then he hopped out of the garden and ran to a thick gorse bush a little way off on the common. There was a rabbit-hole there, and he popped down it.

Soon old Brer Rabbit was making a new burrow. The other rabbits came around and stared in surprise.

"Brer Rabbit! What's the excitement? You don't want to make a burrow near to Brer Fox's house! It's dangerous! When that fox is thin and hungry he may squeeze himself down a burrow and chase us!"

"You leave me to mind my own business," grinned Brer Rabbit, scraping away with his front feet, and sending showers of earth out with his back feet, so that the watching rabbits blinked their eyes and shook the dust out of their ears. Brer Rabbit said no more. He just went on burrowing and burrowing. He knew the way he was going all right—straight for Brer Fox's cellar!

All this time Brer Fox was pulling his carrots, and wheeling them to his house. He opened his trap-door and tipped the carrots down into his dark cellar. Then back he went again for another load of carrots. He went on until he had tipped every carrot into his cellar. Then he wiped his hot forehead, took a drink of lemonade, and locked the padlock on his trap-door. He put the key into his pocket and buttoned it up.

"Well, if old Brer Rabbit can get my carrots now, he's cleverer than I think he is," said Brer Fox, and he got undressed and went to bed, for he was really very tired.

Now it didn't take Brer Rabbit very long to burrow right into Brer Fox's cellar. Pretty soon his head poked through a hole in the floor, and carrots began to fall into the burrow he had made. Brer Rabbit got his teeth into two or three, and mighty good they tasted! He stuffed as many as he could get into the basket he had brought with him, and scurried off home with them.

Then back he came with all his family, every one of them with baskets too, and, my goodness, what a hole they made in that cellarful of carrots! Soon Brer Rabbit's shed was overflowing with the red roots, and old Mrs. Rabbit was dancing a jig of joy to think of the carrot-soup they would have that winter.

"Old Brer Fox, he said I was welcome to any carrots I could get from his cellar," said Brer Rabbit truthfully to his wife. "So we might as well take what we can get, wife."

They didn't stop working till they had taken every single carrot—but just as they were filling the last basket one of the children giggled and awoke Brer Fox. He heard a noise in his cellar, and he felt for his key at once.

Ah! There it was, safe in his pocket. Then what could that noise be in the cellar?

"My!" said Brer Fox suddenly. "I guess I know what it is! Old Brer Rabbit must have hopped down into my cellar just before I tipped my carrots in! And he's sitting there now, nibbling them! Well, he'll be sorry in the morning, for I'll open the trap-door, jump down, and get him as sure as I've got whiskers! Rabbit-pie and carrots and parsley-sauce will be a nice supper to-morrow!"

Brer Fox got up and went to the trap-door. He didn't open it, but he rapped on it hard just to make Brer Rabbit sit up.

"Heyo, Brer Rabbit!" yelled Brer Fox. "I can hear you down there all right! You wait till to-morrow morning—I'll get you then, and you'll be sorry. Till then you're welcome to as many carrots as you like!"

Brer Rabbit grinned round at his family. Then he put on a very scared sort of voice, and answered Brer Fox.

"Mercy, Brer Fox, mercy! Let me go in the morning! Mercy!"

"Ha! You can just sit there all night and think of what's going to happen to-morrow!" said Brer Fox, pleased. He got back into bed and fell asleep.

Brer Rabbit and his family disappeared down the burrow—and then Brer Rabbit filled up the hole he had made into the cellar, and left everything neat and tidy. Back they all went, locked up their carrots, and tumbled into bed to fall asleep in half a minute!

In the morning Brer Fox went to unlock his cellar door, pleased to think he had caught Brer Rabbit at last! He went down a few steps and then shut the trap-door down, for he didn't mean Brer Rabbit to skip out of it.

But tails and whiskers! When poor Brer Fox looked into his cellar, what did he see? Nothing! Nothing at all! Not a carrot. Not a rabbit. It was quite empty.

Brer Fox couldn't believe his eyes! He sat on the steps and looked and looked, wondering if he was in a dream.

And then he heard a small noise above him, and he shot up the steps at once—but he was too late! Brer Rabbit had locked the trap-door with the key that Brer Fox had left on the floor nearby! Brer Fox was a prisoner!

"Brer Fox!" called Brer Rabbit cheekily. "I hope you'll enjoy your carrots!"

"Brer Rabbit, they're gone!" said Brer Fox, more puzzled than he had ever been in his life.

"Yes, I took them," said Brer Rabbit. "You said I was

welcome to any I could take, didn't you now, Brer Fox?"

Then Brer Fox went quite mad with rage and banged on the trap-door as if he'd break it in two.

"Now, now!" said Brer Rabbit. "What a naughty temper! I'm just going, Brer Fox, so good-bye."

"You unlock me, Brer Rabbit!" shouted Brer Fox. "Do you want me to starve in here?"

But Brer Rabbit was gone with a hoppitty skip! Brer Fox was left in the dark cellar, puzzling and wondering how Brer Rabbit could have got there and taken all the carrots when the trap-door was locked.

And there he had to stay till the next day, when Brer Bear came a-calling and was mighty scared to hear Brer Fox wailing in the cellar! Brer Bear unlocked the trap-door, for Brer Rabbit had left the key, and out came Brer Fox, hungry and thirsty, but so angry that he couldn't either eat or drink. He wanted to rush off and catch Brer Rabbit at once, but Brer Bear calmed him down.

"Now, Brer Fox, don't be rash," he said. "If Brer Rabbit can play you such a trick as this, he's too mighty clever for you—so just you sit quiet and wait your time!"

And that's what poor Brer Fox did, whilst Brer Rabbit and his family feasted on carrot-soup and grew as fat as butter all the winter through!

Brer Wolf gets into More Trouble

NOW BRER RABBIT was mighty careful to keep away from Brer Wolf after he had pretended the meat was poisoned, but one day he met him right in the very middle of the big road. Brer Rabbit rushed off to the side, but Brer Wolf shouted to him.

"Whoa there, Brer Rabbit! Don't be in such a hurry! Aren't you ashamed of yourself for the way you tricked me about that meat?"

"Bless gracious, so it's you, Brer Wolf, is it?" said Brer Rabbit, pretending that he hadn't known it was Brer Wolf. "How's yourself and all your folks?"

"You'll find out how they all are before the day's ended!" said Brer Wolf, with a nasty sort of grin. "You took that meat, Brer Rabbit and now I'm a-going to take *you*!"

With that Brer Wolf made a dash at Brer Rabbit, but he just wasn't quite quick enough, and Brer Rabbit went galloping through the woods, lippitty-clippitty, clippitty-lippitty! Brer Wolf shot after him, and there they went—first Brer Rabbit a-scampering and then Brer Wolf a-scooting! Brer Rabbit was faster than Brer Wolf, but Brer Wolf could run for longer, and soon he was so near Brer Rabbit that Brer Rabbit had to run into a hollow log that lay on the ground.

Now Brer Rabbit had been in that log before, and he knew quite well there was a hole at the other end for him to get out of, so he just shot through the log at top speed. He galloped in at one end and out at the other. He didn't stop to say good-bye—no, he just kept on going!

Well, when Brer Wolf saw Brer Rabbit run into that hollow log, he was mighty pleased. Brer Wolf didn't know

there was a hole at the other end. " Heyo ! " said Brer Wolf to himself, " we've been thinking you're mighty cunning all this time, Brer Rabbit, and here you've gone and put yourself into a fine trap ! I've got you this time ! "

Then Brer Wolf laughed, and laid himself down by the end where Brer Rabbit went in, and he panted and got back his breath. Not far off he saw Brer Bear burning up some rubbish, and he shouted to him and asked him to bring a chunk of fire. Brer Bear brought along a burning branch, and they set fire to the hollow log, and sat by it and watched it till it was all burnt up. Then they shook hands solemnly.

" Huh ! " said Brer Wolf, " that's the end of Brer Rabbit."

" And now maybe we'll have some peace in this neighbourhood ! " said Brer Bear.

Now not long after that Brer Wolf thought he would call and tell Miss Meadows about Brer Rabbit. So off he set, all got up in his best things. And when he got there, who should he see sitting up there by one of the girls but old Brer Rabbit himself!

Well, Brer Wolf was certain he had burnt Brer Rabbit in that hollow log, and he stared at him as if he couldn't make him out at all. He was so scared and surprised that he nearly turned tail and ran for home. But his legs just wouldn't take him and he had to sit down and say "how-do-you-do" as politely as he could.

Brer Rabbit bowed to Brer Wolf and shook hands with him just as if nothing had even happened between them.

"Ah-yi, Brer Wolf!" said Brer Rabbit. "You did me a good turn the other day, and I'm so grateful to you that if ever you want a friend, you can count on me!"

"How's that, Brer Rabbit?" said Brer Wolf, astonished. "You've changed your mind pretty quickly."

"And a good thing too," said Brer Rabbit, grinning so kindly at Brer Wolf that he felt really puzzled.

"Why did you change your mind?" said Brer Wolf.

"Why, I'm so pleased that you tried to burn me up in that hollow log, Brer Wolf," said Brer Rabbit. "And when you get time, I wish you'd burn me up some more!"

"How so, Brer Rabbit?" said Brer Wolf, more and more astonished.

"I don't like to tell you, Brer Wolf, in case the news gets round," said Brer Rabbit.

"I won't tell a soul," said Brer Wolf. "You tell me the secret, Brer Rabbit, and I won't tell even my old woman."

Then Brer Rabbit got close to Brer Wolf and spoke into his ear as if he didn't want any one else to hear what he was saying.

"I found out something, Brer Wolf, when you were a-burning me in that hollow log. Do you know that when you get into a hollow tree and some one sets it a-fire, the natural honey just oozles out of it, and after you've sucked in what you want, the honey runs all over you and then it's no use for the fire to try and burn you, because it can't get through the coat of honey? I do hope you'll try and burn me up again, Brer Wolf, because I know where there is a good hollow tree."

Well, Brer Wolf was mighty astonished to hear this. He looked at Brer Rabbit and Brer Rabbit looked back at him as if there was a fine secret between them. Brer Wolf felt sure that what Brer Rabbit was saying must be true, because hadn't he, Brer Wolf, set fire to that hollow log himself?

"I'd like to set out right now and find that hollow tree," said Brer Wolf.

"Good!" said Brer Rabbit. "That's just what I hoped."

So off they went, and it wasn't long before they came to the hollow log that Brer Rabbit said he had picked out. Well, when they got there, Brer Wolf didn't see why Brer Rabbit should sit in the hollow log and eat up the honey. He was greedy for a taste of the honey himself.

"You let *me* get into the hollow tree, Brer Rabbit," he begged. "You've had your turn."

"No, I want another turn," said Brer Rabbit.

"You give me a turn first, and you shall have another turn afterwards," said Brer Wolf.

"All right," said Brer Rabbit. "I'm not the man to say no to my friends when they ask me a favour. You get into the tree, Brer Wolf."

So Brer Wolf squeezed himself in, he did, and Brer Rabbit stuffed up the hole with dry leaves and rubbish, and he grinned to himself, because he knew there wasn't any hole at the other end this time! Then Brer Rabbit got a chunk of fire and set light to the log. It smoked and it smoked, and then burst out into a blaze.

Brer Rabbit piled up bracken and branches and sticks and stones so that Brer Wolf couldn't get out. Soon Brer Wolf began to yell.

"It's getting mighty hot, Brer Rabbit, and I haven't seen any honey yet!"

Brer Rabbit piled on more leaves and shouted back: "Don't be in such a hurry, Brer Wolf! You'll see the honey in a minute, and taste it too!"

The fire burnt up, and the wood popped like pistol-shots. Brer Wolf began to scramble round a bit, and yelled out: "It's getting hotter and hotter, Brer Rabbit. No honey has come yet!"

"Keep still, Brer Wolf—it'll come!"

"Give me some air, Brer Rabbit. I'm a-cooking!"

"Fresh air will turn the honey sour, Brer Wolf. Just keep still!"

"Ow! It's getting hotter and hotter, Brer Rabbit!"

"Just keep still, Brer Wolf! It's nearly time for the honey."

"Ow! Ow! I'm a-cooking, Brer Rabbit!"

"Wait for the honey, Brer Wolf!"

"I can't stand it, Brer Rabbit!"

"Well, you made *me* stand it, Brer Wolf—so just you stand it too! I'll give you honey, Brer Wolf—yes, the same kind as you gave me!"

But poor Brer Wolf couldn't stop in the log looking for honey any longer. He burst right out of it, he did, with sparks a-flying from his fur. And he was so hot that Brer Rabbit felt scorched and took to his heels as if Cousin Wildcat was after him and all his family too!

And after that Brer Wolf kept right away from Brer Rabbit. He'd been scalded—and squashed under a rock—and nearly cooked—and Brer Wolf reckoned Brer Rabbit was just a bit too clever for him!

Brer Rabbit and the Swing

ONCE, WHEN Brer Rabbit was nibbling carrots in Mister Man's garden, Mister Man came along and caught him neatly by the ears. He swung him up into the air and cried, "Ha! Here's the fellow that eats my greens! Here's the fellow that nibbles my carrots!"

"Please, sir, I'll never do it again," squealed Brer Rabbit, his nose trembling up and down with fright.

"You're right there—you never will!" said Mister Man, with a grin, and he tucked Brer Rabbit under his arm and walked off down the garden with him.

Soon he came to where his little girl was swinging up and down on her swing. She stopped swinging and called out, "What have you got, Daddy?"

"I've got the fellow that eats my greens!" said Mister Man, and he swung Brer Rabbit by his ears again. Brer Rabbit hated it. Just then a boy in the next field shouted to Mister Man.

"Hey! Can you come here a minute, sir?"

"Coming!" shouted Mister Man. He stuffed poor Brer Rabbit into a wooden hutch nearby and spoke to his little girl. "Now listen to me—whatever you do, don't let Brer Rabbit out of that hutch. No matter what he says to you, don't you let him out. See?"

"I promise I won't, Daddy," said the little girl, and she went on swinging. Brer Rabbit heard the door of the hutch slammed, and saw Mister Man run off to the next field.

"I'll be back in five minutes," said Mister Man, "and then Brer Rabbit will be in a bad way!"

As soon as Mister Man was gone, Brer Rabbit spoke to the

little girl. " That's a fine swing you've got, little girl ! " he said.

" Yes," she said. " My Daddy made it for me. It goes very, very high—so high that I can see right over the wall into the next field, where there are lots of rabbit-burrows."

" Are there really ? " sighed Brer Rabbit, wishing and wishing that he was down a burrow. " Oh, little girl, wouldn't I just love a swing on your swing ! Do let me have a turn. You could push me very high and I wouldn't be afraid."

" My Daddy said I mustn't let you out of the hutch," said the little girl, swinging to and fro.

" But, little girl, it wouldn't matter if you let me have a swing," said Brer Rabbit. " I could jump back into the hutch as soon as your Daddy came back."

" I dare say you could," said the little girl. " But I promised Daddy I wouldn't let you out of the hutch."

" Little girl, I think you are very selfish," said Brer Rabbit, turning up his nose at her. " You want your swing all to yourself, that's why you won't let *me* have a turn. And I've never, never had a swing in my life. I do think you might let me."

" I told Daddy I wouldn't let you out of the hutch," said the little girl. " But I tell you what I will do for you, Brer Rabbit, just to show you that I am *not* selfish about my swing—I'll ask my Daddy to let you have a turn when he comes back."

"All right," said Brer Rabbit. "But he won't let me. You'll see."

Just then Mister Man came back, and he was pleased to see Brer Rabbit still in the hutch. "You're a good little girl," he said to his small daughter. "You have kept guard on that wicked rabbit very well. What shall I give you for a reward?"

"Oh, Daddy, will you let the rabbit have a turn on my swing?" asked the little girl eagerly. "He says he has never been on a swing. Maybe it's the last thing he'll ever do, so you might let him do it—just to please me!"

"Well," said Mister Man, rather doubtfully, "I'll only let him if *I* put him on the swing and *I* take him off—or he may skip away!"

"Oh, please, Mister Man, you can put me on and take me off yourself," cried out Brer Rabbit in a pleased voice. "Oh, you are very kind to let me have a swing! If *you* put me on and take me off, I can't skip away, can I?"

Mister Man opened the hutch door and took out Brer Rabbit by the ears. He set him on the swing and then began to push him high.

"Oh, higher still, higher still!" cried Brer Rabbit in a delighted voice. "This is lovely!"

The little girl pushed Brer Rabbit higher and higher. He swung to and fro, his whiskers waving as he went. At last

he swung so high that he could see right over the wall and into the next field.

And then old Brer Rabbit jumped! Yes—he waited till the swing was very high, almost over the wall, and then he leapt right off it, over the wall, into a bramble bush, and before anyone could say "Jack Robinson!" he was gone, and the swing was empty.

"He's gone!" cried Mister Man. "Where did he go? Quick! Look for him!"

But though they looked and looked they didn't find old Brer Rabbit. He couldn't have jumped over that wall if he hadn't been swung so high—and he was down a burrow giggling to think of Mister Man's face when he suddenly saw that the swing was empty!

"It's a pity Mister Man didn't feel in my pockets!" said Brer Rabbit, and he took out three large carrots and began to nibble them. "Poor Mister Man—he's no match for Brer Rabbit!"

Brer Rabbit and the Snake

BRER BEAR had a field in which grew the very finest mushrooms that anybody could ever see. They came up every September, and each year Brer Bear invited his friends to come along and help themselves.

But one year he didn't ask Brer Rabbit, and Brer Rabbit was mighty upset.

" Brer Bear, I like mushrooms as much as ever I did," said Brer Rabbit boldly to Brer Bear when he met him.

" But I don't like *you* as much as ever I did ! " said Brer Bear smartly. " No, Brer Rabbit—you've played too many tricks on me and my friends lately. You can go without your mushrooms this year. I and all the others are going mushrooming to-morrow morning, and unless you want to be caught and cooked with the mushrooms, you keep away."

Brer Rabbit was angry—and when he was angry his brain worked very quickly. He nodded to Brer Bear and ran off, thinking hard. He went to the mushroom-field and looked around.

Each year after the mushrooming all the creatures used to sit under a big willow tree which cast a pleasant shade, and there they ate an early breakfast. Brer Rabbit looked very hard at this elm tree and at the burrows around.

" Yes," grinned old Brer Rabbit to himself. " Just as I thought. This willow tree has a nice hollow inside—and there's a burrow the other side that I can slip down. Good ! I'll join the mushrooming party tomorrow morning in a way they won't like."

So the next morning, very early even before the creatures had arrived to pick mushrooms, Brer Rabbit skipped up and hid inside the hollow tree. He waited there, peeking out through a tiny hole to see what was happening.

It wasn't long before Brer Bear ambled up with Brer Coon. Then came Brer Fox with Brer Wolf. Brer Terrapin came and Brer Turkey-Buzzard, and even Cousin Wildcat ran up with a bag, and said how-do to all the rest.

"We're all here," said Brer Bear, "so we'll begin. You take the north end of the field, Brer Fox and Brer Wolf. You have the south, Cousin Wildcat. You have this end, Brer Terrapin and Brer Buzzard—and I and Brer Coon will have the east end."

They all set off. Soon Brer Rabbit could see them bending down, picking the creamy-coloured mushrooms, and it wasn't very long before all the baskets were full.

Then back all the creatures came to sit in the shade under the willow tree. It had been hot in the morning sun. They were glad to undo Brer Bear's picnic bag and take out the cool lemonade and the sandwiches he had packed there. Soon they were all eating and talking.

"It's a good thing we haven't got that rascal of a Brer Rabbit," said Brer Fox, eating a sandwich. "He would somehow manage to get all the finest mushrooms for himself. It's best to leave him out of things like this."

"Well, he won't get a single mushroom *this* year!" said Brer Bear, grinning. "I met him the other day and I gave him such a scolding! My, the things I said to him!"

Brer Rabbit was listening in the tree behind. He thought it was about time for the fun to begin. So he made a soft hissing noise. Only Cousin Wildcat heard it at first and pricked up his ears at once.

Brer Rabbit hissed again, more loudly. This time every one heard it.

"A snake!" said Brer Fox, looking all round.

"I heard it before," said Cousin Wildcat.

"I hate snakes," said Brer Bear.

Brer Rabbit grinned and did a lot more hissing. He really was very good at being a snake. The others looked uncomfortable, and stopped talking to keep a watch out for the snake.

Brer Rabbit slipped out of the hollow tree at the other side, popped down the nearby burrow, came up under a bramble bush and rushed at top-speed towards the other creatures.

"Save me, save me!" yelled Brer Rabbit.

"Now, what's the matter, what's the matter?" cried Brer Bear.

"Snakes!" yelled Brer Rabbit. "Snakes! A whole army of them over the hedge there! Do you mean to say you haven't heard them hissing? Well, I'm off!"

He shot down a burrow, came up by the willow tree again, crept quietly inside and hissed loudly. All the creatures got a fright and jumped up, thinking that the snakes were coming through the hedge!

"Run!" shouted Brer Bear. "Leave everything—we can come back when the snakes have gone."

So every one rushed off to the nearby wood—all except Brer Terrapin, who was a slowcoach, and preferred to put himself inside his shell and pretend to be a stone.

No sooner had everyone gone than Brer Rabbit hopped out of the willow tree and picked up the baskets of mushrooms. He slapped Brer Terrapin on the shell.

"Heyo, old friend!" he grinned. "Just you stay with your head inside your shell, whilst I put all these mushrooms into the hollow tree. Then you and I will have a fine feast this evening. Don't you see anything, Brer Terrapin! All you must do is to hear!"

And with that Brer Rabbit began to hiss like a dozen snakes at once as he tipped the baskets into the hollow tree, and then threw them on the ground, empty.

Brer Terrapin didn't say a word nor did he put his head out of his shell. He just shook a little as if he were laughing. Brer Rabbit hopped down a burrow.

Soon the others all came back, looking around fearfully for the snakes—but all they found was a collection of empty baskets! They spoke to Brer Terrapin, whose head was still under his shell.

"Brer Terrapin! What happened? Did you see anything?"

"Not a thing!" said Brer Terrapin truthfully. "But I heard plenty. My, the hissing there was!"

"The snakes have taken our mushrooms!" groaned Brer Bear. "The thieves! The robbers! Well, we must come again when next the mushrooms are up. I'm sorry, folks—but who'd guess that any army of snakes would come along like that?"

That evening Brer Rabbit and Brer Terrapin took all the mushrooms from the hollow tree and carried them home in sacks. On the way back they met old Brer Bear, and he looked at them mighty queerly when he saw a mushroom fall out of a sack.

"Where did you find those mushrooms?" he asked.

"In a hollow tree," said Brer Rabbit at once.

"Mushrooms don't grow in hollow trees," said Brer Bear, very suspiciously.

"Thank you for telling me!" said Brer Rabbit, and he and Brer Terrapin went in at his front gate, giggling so loudly that Brer Bear knew there was a trick somewhere. But what it was he could NOT think! Poor Brer Bear!

Brer Rabbit's Sausages

ONCE IT happened that Brer Rabbit went to the butcher's and bought a fine string of fat sausages. He was mighty pleased with them, and went home through the woods, lippitty-clippitty, singing a little song.

And who should meet him but Brer Fox and Brer Bear, both looking mighty glum, for they had been fishing and hadn't caught so much as a minnow.

Brer Rabbit ran right into them, and they held him fast.

"Now, now, what are you running away from?" said Brer Fox. "Have you been stealing those sausages?"

"Indeed I haven't," said Brer Rabbit. "I'm an honest fellow, I am! I don't steal sausages."

"Brer Bear, don't you think we ought to take these sausages away from him?" said Brer Fox, winking at Brer Bear. "We'd better take them back to the butcher and see if Brer Rabbit has paid for them."

"Of course I've paid for them," said Brer Rabbit angrily. But he was glad to escape from Brer Fox and Brer Bear, even if it meant leaving his beautiful sausages behind. He edged away from them—and then suddenly ran under a bush and down a hole.

"Ho ho!" laughed Brer Fox. "We've caught no fish, Brer Bear—but we've caught some fine sausages instead! Come along—we'll go to your house and cook them."

Well, Brer Rabbit heard what was said and he was very angry. He skipped out of the hole as soon as he saw Brer Fox and Brer Bear going off—and he followed behind them all the way.

They went into Brer Bear's house. Brer Bear lighted a fire to cook the sausages, and Brer Rabbit saw the smoke coming out of the chimney. He sat by the gate and thought hard.

Outside the front door stood the fishing-rods and lines, left there by Brer Bear and Brer Fox. Brer Rabbit grinned a little and smacked his leg softly. If he didn't get back those sausages, his name wasn't Brer Rabbit!

He slipped along to the front door. He took one of the fishing-rods. He crept round to the back and stood on the big water-butt there. He climbed from that on to the roof and scrambled quietly up to the chimney that was smoking.

Brer Rabbit put his head down it and sniffed. Yes—he could smell those sausages cooking all right! He set a hook on the end of the fishing-line and unwound it. He dropped the hook gently down the chimney till it stopped falling, and he knew it had reached the frying-pan.

Brer Bear had put the sausages into the pan of fat without cutting the string that bound them to one another. There they lay in the pan, a nice string of sizzling sausages! Brer Bear and Brer Fox were laying the table.

"A plate for you and a plate for me," Brer Rabbit heard Brer Bear say. He jerked his line about, trying to catch the hook into the string of sausages—and at last it caught!

Brer Rabbit grinned. He wound up the line. The sausages came up the chimney, getting a bit sooty as they went. But Brer Rabbit didn't mind that. Oh no—a little soot was nothing to him!

The sausages came right out of the chimney. They were mighty hot, so Brer Rabbit took a clean handkerchief from his pocket and spread it on the roof. He put the sizzling sausages there and waited for them to cool. They were just nicely cooked.

He stood up and cocked one ear over the chimney. "One mug for you, one mug for me," he heard Brer Bear say. And then he heard an angry yell.

"Hie, Brer Fox! Where are those sausages? They're not in the pan!"

There was a moment's surprised silence. Then Brer Fox spoke up. "*You've* taken those sausages, Brer Bear. I haven't touched them, I know that. You've taken them out of the pan when I wasn't looking. Where are they?"

"That's what *I* should like to know!" cried Brer Bear angrily. "You just put them back in the pan, Brer Fox, or I'll squeeze you to bits!"

Brer Fox shouted in rage—and then Brer Rabbit heard the two of them rushing round and round the kitchen trying to hit one another.

Crash! Down went a kettle! Clang! Down went three saucepans! Thud! Over went a chair! Smash! The kitchen table overturned. My, there was a fine old to-do in Brer Bear's kitchen that day! Brer Rabbit got so excited about it that he did a little dance up there on the roof and nearly fell off.

Then out rushed Brer Fox, with Brer Bear after him. They ran down the path and into the woods, both yelling and howling fit to wake a hundred sleepers.

Brer Rabbit did enjoy it all. He sat up there on the roof chewing those sausages, and grinning to himself.

And when at last the two of them came back from the woods, hungry, tired, and sore, what did they see but Brer Rabbit sitting up on the roof waving to them.

"I've saved you the sausage skins!" shouted Brer Rabbit, and he threw them at Brer Bear, smack! Then down he jumped to the water-butt and set off home as fast as his legs could carry him—but every now and again he stopped and rolled on the ground with laughter. Oh, he's a comic fellow is Brer Rabbit, no doubt about that!

Brer Rabbit and Wattle Weasel

One time most of the creatures were living in the same house and using the same stream for water. They were all very fond of butter, and they used to keep it all in a cool dairy, taking it when they wanted it.

But one day they found that someone had been nibbling at their butter. So they took it and hid it up in the rafters of the dairy, but the thief found it there and nibbled it. Then they hid the butter in the sand, but when they went to get it, it was half gone, just the same!

Well, the creatures just simply didn't know what to do about it. If Brer Rabbit had been living with them, maybe he'd have put the matter right at once, for there wasn't any creature could trick Brer Rabbit once he set his mind to beating them. But Brer Rabbit wasn't living with them, for they wouldn't have anything to do with him; he had tricked them so often!

"Well," said Brer Wolf, "we'd better find out first who the thief is, and then maybe we can catch him. Let's look at the tracks he makes." So they looked at them, and Brer Fox knew whose tracks they were—they were Wattle Weasel's, sure enough!

So they watched out for him—but he came in the day and he came in the night, and they never got a sight of him at all, he was so cunning.

"We'd better let someone sit in the dairy and watch the butter," said Brer Fox. "Wattle Weasel won't dare to come nibbling at the butter if one of us is there on guard."

Brer Mink was the first one told to watch the butter. The other creatures went off to work, and Brer Mink, he sat up with the butter. He watched and he listened, he listened and he watched. He didn't see anything, he didn't hear anything. But he watched without stopping, all the same, because the rule was that if Wattle Weasel came and got the butter when anyone was on guard, the creature on guard shouldn't get any butter for a year!

So Brer Mink watched and waited. He sat so still that by and by he got cramp in the legs, and just about then Wattle Weasel popped his head under the door. He saw Brer Mink and he shouted to him.

"Heyo, Brer Mink! You look sort of lonesome in there! Come out and have a game of hide-and-seek!"

Well, Brer Mink was just about tired of sitting still, and he wanted a bit of fun—and, after all, if he was playing hide-and-seek with Wattle Weasel, Wattle Weasel couldn't eat the butter! So he joined Brer Mink and began to play. Well, they played and they played, and they ran and they ran till by and by Brer Mink got so worn out that he begged Wattle Weasel to sit down and rest a while.

So they sat down—and so tired was poor old Brer Mink that no sooner did he sit down to rest than he fell fast asleep! Little Wattle Weasel, he wasn't tired out at all, so in he went, nibbled up the butter and popped out the way he came in!

Well, when the creatures came back from their work, they found the butter eaten and Wattle Weasel gone. With that they flew into a rage and told Brer Mink he'd have no butter for a year. Then they picked someone else to guard the butter.

This time it was Brer Possum. He sat down in the shed and grinned and watched and watched and grinned, and by and by, sure enough, in popped little Wattle Weasel. He came in, he did, and he ran right over to Brer Possum and gave him a poke in the ribs. "How are you, old Brer Possum?" he shouted, and gave Brer Possum a few more pokes. Now Brer

Possum was mighty ticklish, and every time Wattle Weasel poked him in the ribs he laughed.

Wattle Weasel tickled him again and he laughed worse than ever, and when Wattle Weasel tickled him with both paws poor Brer Possum laughed till he cried, and he rolled on the floor and shrieked till he hadn't got a bit of breath left. And Wattle Weasel left him rolling there out of breath, and ran to nibble up the butter.

When the creatures came home from work they stared at the nibbled-up butter in a rage. "No more butter for you for a year, Brer Possum," said Brer Wolf. "Who shall we put on guard now? Brer Coon, you sit in here and watch the butter."

So Brer Coon sat in the dairy with the butter. Whilst he was sitting there in came little Wattle Weasel.

"Heyo, Brer Coon!" he cried. "Come for a race down to the stream and back?"

Well, Brer Coon was always one for a race, so off he went—and Brer Coon reckoned that if he could catch Wattle Weasel, the creatures would all be mighty pleased with him when he came home!

But on the way back Wattle Weasel took some short cuts he knew—and left old Brer Coon far behind! Wattle Weasel

nipped into the dairy, popped over to the butter-pail and nibbled it up!

"No butter for *you* for a year!" said Brer Bear to poor Brer Coon that night. "It's time someone really smart was put on guard. Brer Fox, you sit here and watch the butter tomorrow."

So Brer Fox sat in the dairy, watching and waiting for Wattle Weasel. Now, Wattle Weasel was really frightened of Brer Fox, and he sat outside the door and wondered how he could trick him. He didn't dare to go into the dairy with Brer Fox there.

At last Wattle Weasel thought of an idea. He waited till it was dark and then he went to the fields and woke up some pheasants sleeping there. He drove the birds towards the dairy, and Brer Fox heard them outside, squawking. His mouth began to water, for he loved a fat pheasant. By and by he said to himself that it wouldn't matter if he slipped outside and took just one pheasant. So Brer Fox slipped out, and Wattle Weasel, he slipped in, and, bless gracious! The butter was all nibbled up again!

Well, the creatures really didn't know what to do next. So they put Brer Wolf on guard. Brer Wolf sat there and sat there, and almost nodded off to sleep with waiting. By and by he heard someone talking outside the dairy. He put up his ears and listened.

"Seems as if there are creatures walking by, talking among themselves," said Brer Wolf. Brer Wolf listened hard and heard someone say:

"I wonder who put that young sheep down by the chinkapin tree—and I wonder where old Brer Wolf is! If he smells that sheep, it won't be there by the morning!"

Brer Wolf didn't hear any more—it seemed as if the passers-by had gone on. Brer Wolf forgot that he was supposed to be on guard, and he dashed out of the dairy and down to the chinkapin tree to catch the young sheep. But there was no sheep there—and when he got back Brer Wolf saw that Wattle Weasel had popped in and nibbled up the butter! Then he knew that it was only Wattle Weasel who had been outside, telling a story about the sheep to get Brer Wolf out of the dairy!

Well, that meant Brer Wolf had no butter for a year, and Brer Bear was the next one put on guard. Brer Bear sat up there, he did, and licked his paws and felt mighty grand. By and by Wattle Weasel came in dancing.

"Heyo! Brer Bear!" he shouted out. "How do you feel to-day? I thought I heard you snorting in here, and I just dropped in to see you."

"How?" said Brer Bear, politely, but he kept one eye on Wattle Weasel.

"My!" said Wattle Weasel, "look at your fur, Brer Bear! Wherever have you been? It's all ruffled up!"

With that Wattle Weasel began to stroke Brer Bear's fur down, and then he scratched him along the sides, which Brer Bear simply loved. Brer Bear stretched himself out with a grunt and let Wattle Weasel stroke him and rub him and scratch

him. As long as Wattle Weasel was doing that the butter was safe!

But it wasn't long before Brer Bear was fast asleep, and snoring like a thunderstorm! And, of course, Wattle Weasel nibbled up the butter.

"Now what are we to do?" said Brer Wolf. "If we can't keep guard on our butter ourselves, we're in a very poor way."

"Send for Brer Rabbit," said Brer Coon. "He'll trick Wattle Weasel all right."

"You go and fetch him, Brer Fox," said Brer Wolf.

So Brer Fox set off to fetch Brer Rabbit. He came to his house and knocked on the door.

"Who's there?" said Brer Rabbit.

"Brer Fox," said Brer Fox. "We want you to come along and guard our butter for us, Brer Rabbit. Wattle Weasel keeps on nibbling it up."

"Yes—and you'll nibble *me* up, Brer Fox, as soon as I get inside that dairy!" said Brer Rabbit.

"No, we shan't," said Brer Fox. "We want your help."

"It's a trick to get me caught," said Brer Rabbit, "and I'm not so easily caught, Brer Fox. Go home and don't come knocking at my door again!"

Well, before Brer Rabbit would come, Brer Fox had to go down on his bended knees to him. And at last Brer Rabbit said he would do his best—but the creatures would have to give him half the butter if he caught Wattle Weasel for them. So Brer Fox promised and Brer Rabbit went lippitty-clippitty up to the dairy with him.

The creatures went off to work and left him there. Brer Rabbit took a look round. Then he got some strong string, and hid himself where he could keep his eye on the butter. He hadn't waited long before up came Wattle Weasel. Just as he was going to nibble up the butter Brer Rabbit yelled out loudly.

"Let that butter alone!"

Wattle Weasel jumped back as if the butter had burnt him. He jumped back, he did, and said: "Surely you must be Brer Rabbit?"

"The same!" said Brer Rabbit. "I thought you'd know me, Wattle Weasel. Just let that butter alone."

"Let me have one little taste, Brer Rabbit."

"Just let that butter alone!"

Then little Wattle Weasel said he wanted to run a race. But Brer Rabbit shook his head. "I'm tired," he said.

"Well, let's go outside and play hide-and-seek," said Wattle Weasel.

"I'm too old for such games," said Brer Rabbit.

Wattle Weasel thought of all sorts of other games, and by and by Brer Rabbit thought of one too.

"We'll play tug-of-war," he said. "I'll tie your tail to this end of my string, and you tie mine to the other end, and we'll pull and see who's got the strongest tail."

Little Wattle Weasel knew how feeble Brer Rabbit's tail was —but he didn't know how strong Brer Rabbit's tricks were! So they tied their tails up with string.

"You can stand inside the dairy," said Brer Rabbit, "and I'll stand outside. When I shout, pull hard."

Wattle Weasel was pleased to be left inside the dairy with the butter! He stood there waiting for Brer Rabbit to shout. But Brer Rabbit was busy just for the moment! He quickly untied the string from his tail and tied it fast round a tree-root. Then he grinned to himself and gave a shout.

"Pull, Wattle Weasel, pull! We'll see who has the stronger tail!"

Wattle Weasel pulled—and he pulled—and he pulled! But he couldn't seem to pull Brer Rabbit into the dairy by his tail. Brer Rabbit peeped under the door and laughed to see Wattle Weasel pulling and tugging till his tail nearly came off! At last Wattle Weasel yelled out:

"Come and untie me, Brer Rabbit, because you've won! Your tail is stronger than mine!"

But Brer Rabbit didn't go to untie Wattle Weasel's tail—no, he just sat outside the door, grinning away to himself, waiting for the other creatures to come home.

By and by all the animals came back to see about their butter, for they thought maybe Brer Rabbit had nibbled it up himself. But no—there was the butter in its pail, untouched—and there was Wattle Weasel tied up fast by his tail—and Brer Rabbit sitting quietly outside looking as good as a brand new sixpence!

"*I've got your butter in the pail!*
And Wattle Weasel by the tail!"

sang out Brer Rabbit. And my, what a fuss all the creatures made of him.

"He's just the smartest of us all!" said Brer Coon. Brer Rabbit grinned and took his share of the butter.

"I could have told you that years ago!" he said, and off he went, lippitty-clippitty, through the woods back home.

Brer Rabbit Saves Miss Goose

NOW ONE day when Brer Rabbit was lying snoozing just inside a bramble bush, Brer Fox came along with Brer Bear.

It was a hot day, and Brer Bear wanted a rest. So the two of them sat down beside the bramble bush and began to talk.

Brer Rabbit didn't so much as twitch a whisker. Not he! He knew that Brer Fox could reach a paw into his bush and drag him out as easy as winking. So there he lay and tried not to breathe, in case Brer Fox and Brer Bear heard him.

Brer Fox started to talk about old Miss Goose, who was very fat.

"She keeps her door locked at night," he said, "but I know she opens her window in this hot weather. I'm planning to creep in, Brer Bear, and catch old Miss Goose. My, she's fat!"

"You let me help you, Brer Fox," said Brer Bear at once. "You could never carry Miss Goose away alone. You go in and hit her, and I'll help you to carry her away."

"Well, we'll try to-night," said Brer Fox. "You wait outside the window and I'll throw her out to you. You hurry off with her whilst I tidy up the room and pull the bed together a bit. I guess she'll try to fight me and there'll be feathers all over the place."

Brer Rabbit lay still in the bush and listened to all this. He liked old Miss Goose, and he was angry to hear what Brer Fox planned. As soon as Brer Fox and Brer Bear had gone, he sprang to his feet and ran to his house.

He looked through all his cupboards and drawers to find something he wanted. It was a tiny green thing, made of rubber. Brer Rabbit grinned and put it into his pocket. Then he set off for old Miss Goose's house.

She was hanging up some washing on the line. "Good-day, Miss Goose," said Brer Rabbit. "I've bad news for you. Brer Fox and Brer Bear are going to come and catch you to-night."

"Oh lawks! Oh lawks!" cackled Miss Goose, in a dreadful flurry at once. "What am I to do, what am I to do? I'd get Mr. Dog to come and protect me, but he's gone to see his uncle."

"Now don't you get in such a way about it," said Brer Rabbit. "Just you go and spend the night with your cousin, Miss Feathers, and I'll see that Brer Fox and Brer Bear get such a fright they'll never come near you again!"

"Oh, Brer Rabbit, that's mighty kind of you," said Miss Goose, shaking out her feathers and looking very fat. "I'll go and pack my bag now and rush off this minute! Oh, the wicked creatures! Mind you give them a scare, Brer Rabbit."

"I'll do that!" said Brer Rabbit with a grin. He took the little green rubber thing out of his pocket and showed it to Miss Goose.

"This is an air-balloon," he said. "I had it at Christmas-time. When it blows up, it takes the shape of a big bird. I'll blow it up as big as it will go, and then I'll take one of your night-dresses, Miss Goose, and dress the bird-balloon up in it. I'll put it into your bed to-night, and maybe I'll have some fun when Brer Fox comes along."

"Well, I'll be right back to-morrow," said Miss Goose. She stuffed some things into her old bag and set off down the hill, waddling in a great hurry. Wicked Brer Fox! Wicked Brer Bear! She hoped Brer Rabbit would punish them properly.

Brer Rabbit blew up the balloon. He blew it up mighty carefully, for he didn't want it to burst. When it was almost as big as Miss Goose, he tied up the end tightly. Then he took one of Miss Goose's enormous white night-dresses and dressed the balloon in it. He laughed and laughed, for it was the funniest sight in the world to see a balloon wobbling about the room in one of Miss Goose's white nighties.

Brer Rabbit tied a string to the waist of the night-dress, and then waited for the night to come. He locked the door and opened the window a little, just as Miss Goose always did.

He left the balloon-goose standing in the middle of the floor. He went under the bed with the string. Pretty soon he heard the sound of whispering outside, and he pricked up his ears. He saw Brer Fox's head as Brer Fox peeped in at the window. Then he heard him whisper again.

"Miss Goose is just going to bed," whispered Brer Fox to Brer Bear. "She's standing on the floor in her white night-dress. My, she's fat!"

Brer Rabbit pulled the string he held and the balloon-goose bobbed up and down a bit and seemed to walk here and there. Brer Rabbit had to stuff his paw into his mouth to keep from laughing, for the balloon-goose looked the funniest creature in the world.

"She's walking about the bedroom!" whispered Brer Fox to Brer Bear. "She's just ready to get into bed."

Brer Rabbit pulled the string and the balloon-goose wobbled towards the bed. Brer Rabbit waited till Brer Fox had bobbed down again and then he quickly popped the balloon-goose into the bed, and pulled the clothes over it.

Brer Fox peeped again. "She's got into bed," he whispered. "My, what a hill she makes under the bed-clothes! It's a good thing you came to help me carry her, Brer Bear!"

Brer Fox crept in at the window. He tiptoed to the bed. He had his stick in his hand, and he gave the balloon-goose a great blow with it. It made a funny noise and bobbed up and down in the bed. Brer Rabbit pulled his string and the balloon fell out of bed in its night-dress and wobbled about the floor.

"Oh, so you want to fight, Miss Goose, do you!" cried Brer Fox, surprised that Miss Goose could stand after the hard blow he had given her. "Come on then!"

He hit the balloon-goose, who at once wobbled away. Then Brer Fox caught hold of her and lifted her—and he was filled with astonishment that she was so light. Why, there didn't seem anything of Miss Goose at all! She was as light as a feather!

"And I thought she was so fat and heavy!" said Brer Fox to himself.

Then something happened. Brer Rabbit had a long pin—and he suddenly put out his paw and pricked the balloon-goose.

"BANG!"

The goose went pop with a terrific noise. The wind of the big pop blew Brer Fox over. The goose he thought he was holding went to nothing and fell on top of him. He got all tangled up in the enormous white night-dress, and he thought Miss Goose had shot him and was trying to choke him.

"Let me go, turn me loose!" he yelled. "Turn me loose, let me go!"

He rushed to the window and fell out of it on top of Brer Bear, who was waiting. The night-dress was all round him, and Brer Bear quite thought it was Miss Goose who had fallen out of the window. He caught hold of Brer Fox, nightie and all, and tore off with him.

Brer Rabbit went to the window and watched Brer Fox trying to get away from Brer Bear, who was just as determined to hold him, for he quite thought he had got Miss Goose. Brer Rabbit leaned against the window and laughed till he cried. Tears ran down his nose and fell in a pool on the sill. He just couldn't help it, and every time he thought of the balloon-goose going pop in Brer Fox's arms, he cried with laughter again.

As for old Brer Bear, it was a great surprise to him to find he was holding Brer Fox instead of Miss Goose. He couldn't believe it. He set Brer Fox down on the ground and stared at him.

"What do you want to do this for?" he asked. "Dress yourself up like that in a night-dress and throw yourself into my arms as if you were Miss Goose! Where *is* Miss Goose?"

"She shot me, BANG, BANG!" said Brer Fox, trembling all over as he got himself out of the great night-dress. "Didn't you hear?"

"Ooooh, was that a gun she had?" asked Brer Bear, who was really afraid of guns. "Well, Brer Fox, that's the very last time I go after Miss Goose. Why, she's *dangerous*!"

So Miss Goose is quite safe now, and she came back the next day and settled in happily. As for Brer Rabbit, he kept having laughing fits for weeks—and I don't wonder at it, do you?

You Can't Trick Brer Rabbit

ONCE Brer Rabbit saw Brer Fox, Brer Wolf, and Brer Bear going off to market with their pockets full of money.

"I guess they'll be back this way again this evening," grinned Brer Rabbit to himself. "Well, I'll play a little trick on them and see what they do."

So he got two old brown bean pods, and stuck thistledown on them. When he had finished, the bean pods looked just like two long furry ears.

Brer Rabbit went to a bush beside the road and carefully arranged the two pretend-ears upright behind the bush, so that they stuck up straight like furry rabbit-ears. My, they did look real!

Brer Rabbit ran round the front of the bush and grinned to see the ears. "It looks as if I'm hiding behind the bush, waiting for somebody!" he said.

By that time it was getting on for evening. Brer Rabbit scampered across the road and hid down a burrow there. A piece of bracken hid the entrance. He put his eyes to the bracken, and found that he could see the road beautifully. He sat there and waited, chuckling every time he saw the furry ears opposite him, across the road.

Presently he heard the sound of footsteps coming, and the noise of voices talking loudly. "I hear Brer Bear's deep voice," said Brer Rabbit. "And that's Brer Wolf's growly voice—and yes, that's Brer Fox's barking tone, too."

The voices and the footsteps came nearer—and then they suddenly stopped.

" Look ! " said Brer Fox in a low voice. " Can you see Brer Rabbit's ears sticking up behind that bush, Brer Wolf ? "

" Yes, I can," said Brer Wolf. " If only we could catch him."

" We can't," said Brer Bear. " He'd be off like a shot before we got near him."

" I've got an idea," said Brer Fox. " What about you and Brer Bear pretending to fight one another, Brer Wolf—and then, whilst Brer Rabbit is watching the fight, and not taking any notice of me, I'll slip round the bush quietly and pounce on him from behind."

" That's a fine idea," said Brer Wolf. " And we'll have rabbit-hot-pot for supper ! Come on, Brer Bear— put up your fists and we'll pretend to fight one another ! Brer Rabbit will watch us, and quite forget to keep his eyes on Brer Fox."

Brer Rabbit heard all these whispers, because the others were quite near his burrow. He grinned to himself, and twitched his whiskers in delight.

" Wait a minute," said Brer Bear. " Let me put my parcels down. I've got best butter in there, Brer Wolf, and I don't want it to be squashed by a blow from your great paws ! "

Brer Bear put down his butter. Brer Wolf put down a load of cabbages too. Brer Fox set down two pairs of kippers that smelt most delicious. My, didn't Brer Rabbit's whiskers begin to curl when he smelt them!

"Shout at me, Brer Bear!" whispered Brer Wolf. "Shout something rude. Then I'll rush at you and we'll pummel one another. But don't be too rough."

"Hie, come on, you good-for-nothing, scraggy-tailed wolf!" yelled Brer Bear at once. Brer Wolf gave a most dreadful howl and rushed at Brer Bear. They began to pummel one another —biff—thud—smack!

Brer Rabbit enjoyed it all very much indeed, but he didn't keep his eyes on the fight the whole time. Oh no, he had something else to do as well—he kept his eyes on the butter, the cabbages, and the kippers!

As soon as he saw Brer Fox slipping away from the others, going towards the bush behind which Brer Rabbit had put the pretend-ears, Brer Rabbit put his paw softly out of his burrow.

He pulled the parcel of butter into the hole. He pulled the cabbages, squeezed them beside him and shot them down the burrow. Then he put out his paw for the kippers. Very gently he slid them down the burrow, grinning as he heard the hard smacks that Brer Bear and Brer Wolf were giving one another.

There was a sudden yell from Brer Fox as he pounced on the furry ears, still thinking that they belonged to Brer Rabbit—but he soon gave a different sort of yell when he found that the ears were only pretend-ones! He snatched them up from the bush and tore round to show them to Brer Bear and Brer Wolf.

"Look at this!" he said. "It's only just a pretend pair of ears that Brer Rabbit has put there to trick us."

The others glared at the ears. Brer Wolf opened his mouth, snapped at them, and bit them in half. Then he threw them on the ground.

"I'll snap Brer Rabbit in half when I get him!" he growled. "Here we've been hitting each other all for nothing, Brer Bear and I—all because of that silly pair of ears! I'm going home. Where's my parcel of cabbages?"

Where indeed? Certainly not where he put them.

"What's happened to my butter?" said Brer Bear, glaring at Brer Fox. "Have you eaten our butter and cabbages whilst we've been fighting, Brer Fox?"

"Of course not," said Brer Fox angrily. "*I'd* like to know where my kippers are! You're very fond of kippers, Brer Wolf. Do *you* know anything about them?"

"Look here, Brer Fox, you know quite well that Brer Bear and I have been fighting all this time," said Brer Wolf. "*You're* the only one we weren't watching."

"I'll fight you if you say I've taken your things!" yelled Brer Fox, mighty wild, and he gave Brer Wolf such a slap that it sounded like a clap of thunder! And then, my goodness, there was a *real* fight! Up and down the road went those three animals, slapping and smacking for all they were worth. Brer Rabbit sat in his hole and laughed till the tears came into his eyes and trickled down his whiskers!

At last he poked his ears out of the burrow and called out loudly, "Now, now, folks! That isn't the right way to behave at all! I'm afraid I'll have to take your goods away from you, if you behave like naughty little boys! Thanks for the butter, Brer Bear! Thanks for the cabbages, Brer Wolf—and many, many thanks for the kippers, dear Brer Fox!"

And with that Brer Rabbit disappeared down the burrow at top speed, laughing like a woodpecker.

As for those three animals, they stopped fighting and rushed to the hole together—but it was too late. Brer Rabbit was gone, and their goods were gone too. You simply *can't* trick old Brer Rabbit!

Willy-Waggle-Ears

ONCE Brer Rabbit went to market to buy a sack of vegetables for his family. Brer Fox, Brer Wolf, and Brer Bear got to hear of this, and as it was winter-time, and they were all hungry, they thought they would lie in wait for old Brer Rabbit and catch him.

"Then we'll share out his vegetables between us, and have good soup for a few nights at least," said lean Brer Wolf, licking his lips.

Now Brer Rabbit had to go home through a narrow valley, and when he got there, he stood and sniffed for a minute, with the sack over his shoulders.

"I smell fox," said Brer Rabbit to himself. "And I smell wolf—and what's more, I smell bear too. Now what should fox, wolf, and bear be doing altogether in this narrow valley?"

Well, it wasn't long before old Brer Rabbit guessed they were there waiting for him. So he skipped back over the hill, went all the way round it, and came up not very far behind the three watchers, who were staring down the track in front of them, waiting for Brer Rabbit.

Brer Rabbit popped his sack safely in a cave, and wondered if he should go home—but no, he would give the others a shock first. It would do them good! They were watching for some one to come—all right, some one *would* come, but not the person they thought!

Brer Rabbit went to a bee-tree and got some honey out of it. The bees buzzed angrily, but Brer Rabbit took no notice. He smeared himself with the honey, and then rolled over and over under a big chestnut tree. Soon he was quite covered

with the prickly chestnut cases that stuck tightly to him because of the honey.

"I guess I look like some sort of a hedgehog now!" grinned Brer Rabbit to himself. "What about some new ears for me?"

He went to where some turkey-cocks had been fighting. Long feathers lay about. Brer Rabbit took three or four of the longest, and tied them upright to his ears so that they stuck up high, enormously long and wavy.

He capered about a little. A dormouse saw him and stared in horror. What was this prickly creature with the enormous ears? He gave a squeal and ran away.

"I'm Willy-Waggle-Ears, I'm Willy-Waggle-Ears!" yelled Brer Rabbit, capering about like a mad thing. "I waggle my ears and I jump like a kangaroo!"

He gave such a leap that the dormouse disappeared down

its hole at once. Brer Rabbit gave another leap, and his long ears waggled in the wind in a very strange manner.

Brer Rabbit went leaping and bounding along like this, shouting and yelling all the time. Brer Fox, Brer Wolf, and Brer Bear, who were still watching for Brer Rabbit to come down the valley, turned round in horror.

"What is it? What is it?" cried Brer Fox, clutching tight hold of Brer Wolf.

"I'm Willy-Waggle-Ears! I'm Willy-Waggle-Ears!" yelled Brer Rabbit, leaping high. "I jump like a kangaroo! I eat like an elephant! I fight like a tiger!"

His great feather ears waggled and waved in the wind. Brer Bear was so frightened that he trod on Brer Wolf's foot and squashed it. Brer Wolf gave a yell. That frightened Brer Bear still more, and he tore away, knocking both Brer Fox and Brer Wolf down as he went.

Along came this leaping, bounding creature, its long ears making it seem very tall indeed. Brer Fox began to slink away, but Brer Wolf seemed to think he knew the voice of Willy-Waggle-Ears. Yes—it seemed to him just a bit like the voice of that tricky old Brer Rabbit!

"I'll catch hold of Willy-Waggle-Ears and just see if he's quite such a waggle-ear as he says he is!" said Brer Wolf to himself. So he waited till Brer Rabbit came bounding by—and then he rushed at him.

"I fight like a tiger! I'm full of claws!" yelled Brer

Rabbit as Brer Wolf caught him. "I'll scratch you to bits! I'm full of claws!"

Well, of course, he was covered with prickly chestnut cases, so when Brer Wolf caught hold of him it really did feel to him as if Willy-Waggle-Ears was full of claws. He was pricked all over, and he let Brer Rabbit go very quickly.

"I fight like a tiger, I'm full of claws!" yelled Brer Rabbit, and he chased Brer Wolf all down the valley as fast as he could go. The wind blew off his feather-ears, and the chestnut-cases all fell off too—so in the end Brer Rabbit was just himself, running after old Brer Wolf.

Brer Fox and Brer Bear, who were hiding in the bracken, saw Brer Wolf pounding by, with Brer Rabbit after him. They were most astonished. They looked at one another in dismay.

"Brer Wolf is running away from Brer Rabbit!" said Brer Fox. "Let's not wait for Brer Rabbit any more. If Brer Wolf is frightened of him, we'd better go home!"

So off they went at top speed—and when Brer Rabbit had chased Brer Wolf splash into the river, he went to the cave, took out his sack of vegetables, and went safely home, singing at the top of his cheeky voice:

"I'm Willy-Waggle-Ears! I fight like a tiger! I'm full of claws! I'm old Willy-Waggle-Ears! Make way, make way for old Willy-Waggle-Ears!"

And everybody made way. They were afraid of Willy-Waggle-Ears—yes, and they were afraid of old Brer Rabbit too!

Brer Fox's New Boots

ONCE IT happened that Brer Fox had some money to spend, and he bought himself two pairs of fine strong boots to wear when he went running all the way to his cousin in Hilly Wood.

The first time he put his new boots on to go and see his cousin, he met old Brer Rabbit. My, how Brer Rabbit stared when he saw Brer Fox's brand-new boots! Brer Fox had shined them up beautifully and they shone like coal, all four of them.

"You've got new boots, Brer Fox," said Brer Rabbit.

"I have, Brer Rabbit," said Brer Fox, grinning, and tapping smartly with all four feet on the ground.

"I wonder if they'd fit *me*," said Brer Rabbit, looking at the boots longingly.

"I dare say they would, Brer Rabbit," said Brer Fox, still grinning. "But you're not going to try them! Ha! I know the trick you once played on Mister Dog—tried on all his new shoes, and ran off in them! You won't trick *me* that way. No, Brer Rabbit, I'm as smart as you are, any day!"

"Oh, well," said Brer Rabbit, looking at Brer Fox's feet again, "I'm sure they wouldn't fit me. I've little feet, Brer Fox, and yours are big and clumsy!"

"Indeed they are not!" said Brer Fox. "They are as small as yours; but I'm not going to have a match to see who's got the smallest feet, Brer Rabbit—you'd be away in my new boots before I'd time to measure your feet in them! *I* know you!"

"Brer Fox, you're in a silly mood to-day," said Brer Rabbit, offended. "I'll wish you good-day."

And off he went through the trees, showing his white bobtail as he ran. When he got to an old tree-stump he knew, he sat down and thought about those boots of Brer Fox's. Brer Rabbit meant to get them. But how could he ? He sat and thought, and then he jumped up, slapped his knees and skipped around a bit.

That night, when Brer Fox was quietly sleeping in his bed, dreaming of fat chickens, Brer Rabbit crept into his garden and hid behind a bush.

And then such a noise came from behind that bush ! It was just like a cat-and-dog fight !

" Grrrrrrr ! Me-ow ! Yelp, yelp, yelp ! Ssssssss ! MEEEEE-ow ! Wuff, wuff ! "

Brer Fox woke up with a dreadful jump and sat up in bed, the hairs on his back all standing up straight. Whatever could that noise be ?

" Grrrrrrr ! Ssssssss-SP ! Wuff-wuff ! "

" It's a cat and a dog having a fight ! " said Brer Fox to himself. " Well, I hope they both lose ! Disturbing my sleep like that ! "

He lay down again and shut his eyes. Brer Rabbit began again, and, my goodness, the noises he made ! All the cats and dogs within miles were listening in astonishment !

" Yelp-yelp-grrrrrrr ! Ssssss-sp ! Snarl, snarl ! Wuff-wuff-wuff ! Meeeee-ow, ee-ow-ee-ow-ee-ow ! "

Brer Fox sat up in bed again, very angry. " How can a fellow get to sleep with that noise going on ! " he shouted out of the window. " Be quiet, or I'll throw something at you ! "

" Sssssss-grrrrrrr-WOOF ! " said Brer Rabbit.

Brer Fox looked around for something to throw. He saw his new boots. He picked one up and aimed it carefully at the bush behind which he thought the cat and dog were fighting. Crash ! The boot fell right into the middle of the bush, and

Brer Rabbit grinned. He was well hidden underneath and the boot didn't hurt him. He began again.

" Ssssss-snarl ! Sssssss-snap ! Grrrrrrr ! "

" Stop that noise ! " yelled Brer Fox in a rage, and he threw the second boot. Crash ! Into the bush it went. Brer Rabbit was very pleased. He put the boots on his hind feet. They were a little big, but very comfortable indeed—and so smart ! Now he must get the others.

But Brer Fox was getting so angry that he shouted out that he would come and scare the cat and dog out of his garden, so Brer Rabbit had to be quiet, for he didn't want Brer Fox to find him. He wondered how to get the other pair of boots—and soon it was dawn, and the sky grew pale.

A little bird began to sing sweetly. Brer Rabbit grinned. He left his bush and hopped up on to the rain-barrel. There was a pear tree nearby, and Brer Rabbit jumped into the thick leaves. Then he began to chirrup like a dozen sparrows. My, how he chirrupped !

" Chirry-chirry-chirrup ! Chirp-chirp-chirp-chirp ! Cherry-erry-erry-chirrup ! Chirrrrrrrrrrr ! "

Brer Fox woke up again and frowned. He stuck his head out of the window and yelled up to the pear tree :

" Hey, you Jack Sparrow up there ! Go and chirp somewhere else ! What do you mean by waking a fellow up so early in the morning ? "

" Chirrrrrrrrr-up ! Chirp-chirp-CHIRP ! " answered wicked Brer Rabbit, enjoying himself mightily.

" Didn't you hear what I said ? " shouted Brer Fox. " I'll throw something at you if you don't fly away ! "

" Chirrry-chirry-chirry, CHIRP ! " said Brer Rabbit from the pear tree, and he went on and on like a crowd of noisy sparrows telling each other the news.

Brer Fox gave a yell of rage, picked up a boot and threw it into the pear tree. Brer Rabbit was ready for it and caught it neatly. He chirrupped again, and Brer Fox threw the last boot as hard as ever he could. Brer Rabbit caught it, gave a few frightened chirrups, and swung the leaves about as if a whole crowd of birds were flying away.

Then he sat quite still. Brer Fox was pleased. " Ha ! I got the birds that time ! " he said. " Now perhaps I'll be able to finish my sleep in peace. What a night ! "

Brer Rabbit waited until he could hear loud snores coming through the open window, and then he slipped down the tree and out of the gate. He sat down and put on the other pair of boots ; now he could clippitty-clop down the road as grand as anything ! Off he went, tippitty-tap, clippitty-clop !

And when Brer Fox went to look for his boots after breakfast, there wasn't one to be found. They were quite gone ! He was most astonished—but he was more astonished still when he met old Brer Rabbit out, wearing four shining new boots that looked *very* like the ones Brer Fox had worn the day before.

" Brer Rabbit ! Where did you get those boots ? " cried Brer Fox in a fine rage.

" Now, Brer Fox, now ! " said Brer Rabbit, looking very surprised. " What do you mean ? Can't anyone but you have new boots ? What would you say if you heard that a cat and a dog and some sparrows had given me these boots ? "

And then Brer Fox knew he had been tricked again, and he gave a fierce snarl. Brer Rabbit guessed it was time to run, and he ran—you could hear him all the way down the lane in his big boots—tippitty-tap, clippitty-clop, tippitty-tap !

Brer Bear's Party

ONCE BRER BEAR, Brer Wolf, and Brer Fox got together, and said they'd have a party, and ask Brer Rabbit too.

"You see, Brer Bear, you don't need to get any dinner ready for us if you ask old Brer Rabbit," grinned Brer Fox. "All you'll want will be three plates, three knives and forks, and one good big pot of boiling water ready on the fire!"

"All right," said Brer Bear. "I don't feel very friendly towards Brer Rabbit just now. He's always making fun of me and tricking me. I'm just about tired of him."

"Now don't you tell him that you've asked me and Brer Wolf," said Brer Fox. "Just ask him in to dinner to-morrow, and tell him you've got something special for him. Say you've got hot chestnut-pie. He loves chestnuts."

"You leave it to me. I'll manage Brer Rabbit all right!" said Brer Bear. So he went out to find old Brer Rabbit.

He came to Brer Rabbit's house and knocked on the door, blim-blam, blim-blam!

"Who's there?" asked Brer Rabbit.

"A good friend of yours!" shouted back Brer Bear.

"Good friends ask people out to dinner!" yelled back Brer Rabbit.

"Well, that's just what I've come to ask you!" said Brer Bear. "You come along to dinner with me to-morrow, Brer Rabbit, and I'll have a nice hot chestnut-pie for you!"

Brer Rabbit was astonished to hear such a thing from Brer Bear. He poked his head out of the window and stared at him hard. Brer Bear stared back, and didn't blink an eyelid.

"All right, I'll be along," said Brer Rabbit, and popped his head in again.

Now the more Brer Rabbit thought about Brer Bear, the funnier he thought it was that Brer Bear should ask him to dinner.

"But I'll go," said Brer Rabbit to himself. "Oh yes, I'll go—and I'll come back too, though maybe Brer Bear isn't expecting me to!"

Twelve o'clock was Brer Bear's dinner-time. Brer

Rabbit scuttled along to his house at half-past eleven, just to see what he could see. All he saw from outside was a mighty lot of smoke coming from Brer Bear's chimney.

"That's a mighty big fire to cook a small chest-nut-pie!" said Brer Rabbit, rubbing his chin. "I'll just look in at the window and see what I can see."

So he peeped in, and all he saw was an enormous pot boiling on a big fire, and, on the table, three plates and three knives and forks. Nothing else at all.

"Funny!" said Brer Rabbit. "*Three* plates! I don't like it. No, I don't like it."

He couldn't see anyone in the room at all. Brer Wolf and Brer Fox were hidden behind a curtain, and Brer Bear was waiting by the door.

"Shall I go and knock at the door or not?" wondered Brer Rabbit. "Yes—I'll go—but Brer Bear won't get me indoors. No—I'll take him for a walk that he won't like!"

So Brer Rabbit marched round to the door and knocked loudly on it—BLAM, BLAM, BLAM!

Brer Bear opened it at once, and grinned all over his big mouth.

"Come along in," he said. "The pie is cooking."

"Well, Brer Bear, I hope you've got shrimp sauce with it," said Brer Rabbit, not going indoors. "I surely hope you have. You know, chestnut-pie is nothing without shrimp sauce."

"Well, no, I haven't got shrimp sauce," said Brer Bear. "But you come along in and taste the pie, Brer Rabbit. You won't want shrimp sauce, I know you won't."

"Oh yes, I shall," said Brer Rabbit. "And what's more, I'm not going to eat the pie without shrimp sauce, Brer Bear. If only I'd known you'd got no shrimp sauce I'd have brought you along a whole heap of shrimps myself. There's plenty in the old well not far from here."

"I thought shrimps were only found in the sea," said Brer Bear, astonished.

"Not the sort of shrimps *I'm* talking about!" said Brer Rabbit.

"Well, never mind about shrimps," said Brer Bear, hearing an impatient noise from behind the curtains. "You come in and smell the pie, Brer Rabbit. If you don't like it, you can go."

"I tell you I'm not going to eat any pie without hot shrimp sauce," said Brer Rabbit. "I'll tell you what, Brer Bear!

You get your net and come along with me to the well and fish up a few shrimps. I can't reach down, I'm too short, but you could easily reach with a net."

"Oh, all right, all right!" said Brer Bear. He went indoors and found his net.

A loud whisper came from behind the curtains: "Don't you let Brer Rabbit out of your sight, Brer Bear! Get the shrimps and bring him back at once."

"All right, all right," said Brer Bear, who was beginning to feel that he was doing all the work. He went out of the

house and slammed the door. Then he and Brer Rabbit set off together.

"You see, Brer Bear, nobody who is anybody ever dreams of eating chestnut-pie without shrimp sauce," said Brer Rabbit as they went along. "I'm really surprised that you didn't think of it."

"Oh, you are, are you," said Brer Bear, feeling more and more annoyed. "Well, we'll get the silly shrimps and make them into sauce—though I guess you've got enough sauce of your own without bothering about any extra, Brer Rabbit!"

They came to the well. Brer Bear looked down into the

deep, dark water. He couldn't see a single shrimp, and this was not really surprising, because there wasn't one to see!

"Ah, look! There goes a shrimp—and another—and another!" said Brer Rabbit in an excited voice. "Oooh, look at that fat fellow. Isn't he a lovely red colour!"

"I thought shrimps didn't go red till they were cooked," said Brer Bear, surprised.

"These shrimps are not like the ones you've seen before," said Brer Rabbit firmly. "Quick, Brer Bear—catch them, catch them! Put in your net!"

Brer Bear put in his net, hoping that a few shrimps would swim into it, for he couldn't see a single one to catch. But his net wouldn't quite reach.

"Lean right over, lean right over!" cried Brer Rabbit. "Then your net will reach!"

"Well, hold on to my trousers then," said Brer Bear.

So Brer Rabbit caught hold of the seat of Brer Bear's trousers, and Brer Bear leaned right over to make his net reach the water.

And then suddenly Brer Rabbit let go Brer Bear's trousers—and down he went into the well, splish, splash!

"Oooble, oooble, ooble," gurgled poor Brer Bear, spluttering and choking as he came up again, and floundered about in the water. "Brer Rabbit, you let me go! And just look here—there isn't a single shrimp to be seen! They're not real!"

"They're just as real as your chestnut-pie, Brer Bear!" grinned Brer Rabbit, leaning over the top of the well. "Yes, just as real! Good-bye! I hope you enjoy your bathe!"

He skipped off back to Brer Bear's house, dancing as he went. He poked his head in at the door and yelled to Brer Wolf and Brer Fox:

"Heyo, there! Brer Bear says there are such a lot of shrimps down that well, he wants some help. Hurry along, hurry along!"

Brer Fox and Brer Wolf rushed to the well to get some of the shrimps, but all they saw there was a very wet, very cold, and very angry bear!

"Get him out and give him some of that hot chestnut-pie!" yelled Brer Rabbit, dancing about in the distance. "He can have my share—and tell him he can have sauce from Brer Rabbit, instead of from shrimps! He'll like that, he will!"

And off went Brer Rabbit in delight, stopping every now and again to roll on the ground and laugh like twenty hyenas!

Brer Rabbit Feels Mighty Skittish

ONE MORNING in the autumn Brer Rabbit was skipping about in the woods. The wind blew cool and it made Brer Rabbit feel mighty frisky, and every time the wind rattled in the bushes he jumped this way and that, pretending that he was scared.

He went on this way, hoppetty-skippetty, when by and by he heard Mr. Man cutting a tree down a long way off in the woods. Brer Rabbit stopped, and listened first with one ear and then with the other.

Mr. Man cut and cut and Brer Rabbit, he listened and listened. By and by down came the tree—*kubber-lang-bang-blam!* Well, Brer Rabbit pretended to be so scared that he jumped higher than a brier-bush, and then he leapt out as if the dogs were after him!

Old Brer Rabbit wasn't really scared—he was just having a little game with himself because he felt so mighty skittish that morning. In those days there was nothing in the world that could scare Brer Rabbit. Well, he ran and he ran till he got all out of breath, and just as he was going to stop and get his breath again, who should he meet but Brer Coon, going home after calling on old Brer Bull-Frog. Brer Coon saw Brer Rabbit racing along and he called to him.

"What's your hurry, Brer Rabbit?"

"Haven't time to stop, Brer Coon!"

"Are your folks ill?"

"No, Brer Coon! I haven't time to stop!"

"Trying to see how fast you can run?"

"No, Brer Coon. I haven't time to stop."

"Do, pray, Brer Rabbit, tell me the news."

"Oh, Brer Coon, there's a mighty big fuss back there in the woods—*kubber-lang-bang-blam!* I haven't time to stop!"

This scared Brer Coon because he was far away from his home, and he rushed away and went sailing through the trees as fast as he could. He hadn't gone far before he met Brer Fox. Brer Fox shouted to him in surprise.

"Hey, Brer Coon, where are you going?"

"Haven't time to stop!"

"Are you going for the doctor?"

"No! Haven't time to stop!"

"Do, pray, Brer Coon, tell me the news!"

"Oh, Brer Fox, there's a mighty big fuss back there in the woods—*kubber-lang-bang-blam!* Haven't time to stop!"

Well, when Brer Fox heard that and saw Brer Coon's heels going off through the trees he guessed he'd better run too. So he leapt off into the wind and very soon he met Brer Wolf. Brer Wolf yelled to him.

"Hey, Brer Fox! Stop and rest yourself!"

"Haven't time to stop!"

"Who wants the doctor?"

"No one, Brer Wolf. Haven't time to stop!"

"Do, pray, Brer Fox, tell me the news, good or bad."

"Oh, Brer Wolf, there's a mighty big fuss back there in the woods—*kubber-lang-bang-blam!* Haven't time to stop!"

Brer Wolf was mighty scared to hear all this and he got up and raced off in a fright. Soon he met Brer Bear and Brer Bear shouted to him.

"Hey, Brer Wolf, who's after you?"

"No one, Brer Bear. Haven't time to stop!"

"Well, who are you after then, Brer Wolf?"

"No one, Brer Bear. Haven't time to stop."

"Do, pray, Brer Wolf, tell me the news!"

"Oh, Brer Bear, there's a mighty big fuss back there in the woods—*kubber-lang-bang-blam!* Haven't time to stop!"

Brer Bear gave a snort and ran off too, as scared as could be—and goodness gracious, it wasn't long before every creature in the woods was skaddling through the trees as if a pack of dogs was chasing them—and all because Brer Rabbit heard Mr. Man cut a tree down!

They ran and they ran, and at last they came to Brer Terrapin's house, and they slowed up a bit to get their breath.

"Where are you all going?" asked Brer Terrapin in astonishment.

"Oh, there's a terrible fuss back there in the woods," said the creatures.

"What sort of fuss?" asked Brer Terrapin.

"I don't exactly know," said Brer Coon.

"Nor do I," said Brer Fox. And they all said the same.

"Well, who heard this mighty big fuss?" said Brer Terrapin. But it seemed as if none of the creatures had heard anything at all. This made old Brer Terrapin laugh inside his shell.

"Well, well," he said, "you can all run along if you feel as skittish as all that. But I'm a-going to cook my breakfast and wash up my dishes, and if I hear any mighty big fuss, well, maybe I'll take down my sunshade and come along after you!"

The creatures looked at one another and began to ask who started the news about the mighty big fuss—and they found

out that it was Brer Rabbit who had started the news going—but Brer Rabbit wasn't there! They had all been running for miles, but Brer Rabbit, he hadn't run with them.

"I saw him last," said Brer Coon, "and sure enough he told me what a mighty big fuss there was away in the woods—*kubber-lang-bang-blam!*"

"You shouldn't have listened to him," said Brer Fox.

"And you shouldn't have listened to me, then," said Brer Coon. And then they began to squabble and fight, till Brer Terrapin said that if they wanted to get things straight they had better go and see old Brer Rabbit about it. So off they all went, and when they got to Brer Rabbit's house there he was a-sitting cross-legged in his front porch, winking his eye at the sun.

"What did you trick me for, Brer Rabbit?" grunted Brer Bear.

"Trick who, Brer Bear?"

"Me, Brer Rabbit, that's who!"

"Why, Brer Bear, this is the first time I've seen you to-day!"

Then Brer Fox spoke up.

"What did you trick *me* for, Brer Rabbit? Here I've been

skaddling through the woods till I've got no more breath left to blow my porridge with."

"Why, Brer Fox, it's the first time I've seen you to-day! I wouldn't trick you for the world, Brer Fox, that I wouldn't."

And then Brer Coon spoke.

"What did you trick me for, Brer Rabbit?"

"How did I trick you, Brer Coon?"

"You told me there was a mighty big fuss back there in the woods, Brer Rabbit, and you were rushing away when I saw you, and you said *kubber-lang-bang-blam!*"

"Well, there surely was a mighty big fuss, Brer Coon."

"What kind of a fuss, Brer Rabbit?"

"Ah-yi! You ought to have asked me that before you rushed away and told everybody else," said Brer Rabbit, winking at the sun.

"Well, I'm asking you now, Brer Rabbit."

"I heard Mr. Man cutting a tree down," said Brer Rabbit, "and it made a mighty big fuss when it fell—*kubber-lang-bang-blam!* Ho, yes, and it made me feel mighty skittish, Brer Coon, so I just frisked off like a couple of lambs in the spring."

"Do you mean to say that was the mighty big fuss?" squealed Brer Coon.

"That's so, Brer Coon—and if it set you all skaddling through the woods as if the Wull-of-the-Wust were after you, well, you must have felt mighty skittish too! I wish you good day, folks. Get to bed early this night, for you'll feel mighty tired after your racing about!"

And with that Brer Rabbit knocked his pipe out, winked at the sun and went indoors. All the other creatures snapped their jaws and went slinking off home. Oh! Brer Rabbit was a mighty man in those days, no doubt about that!

Brer Rabbit is a Giant!

NOW ONE time Brer Rabbit went about a good bit with his cousins, Brer Flip and Brer Flop. They were all three as like as peas, and they got into as much mischief as crows in a field of corn!

They took the honey from Brer Bear's pet bee-tree. They found the new peas in Brer Wolf's pea-patch, and didn't they enjoy them! They even dug up a few of Brer Wolf's juicy turnips one night, just to show him they didn't care for *him!*

Well, every one got very tired of Brer Rabbit and his two friends. Brer Wolf was angry about his turnips and he planned to set a watch on them and see that no more were stolen.

So what did he do but put up a big old scarecrow in a long coat and old hat in his turnip-field. Well, when Brer Rabbit and Brer Flip and Flop saw the scarecrow, how they laughed!

"Brer Wolf thinks we're a set of jackdaws, ready to be scared by an old thing like that!" chuckled Brer Rabbit. "We'll show him! We'll dance round the old scarecrow to-night and sing him a song. Then maybe when Brer Wolf hears us, he'll look out of the window and see just how scared we are of his scarecrow!"

But what the three rabbits didn't know was that Brer Wolf himself was in that scarecrow! Yes—inside that long coat was the long body of angry Brer Wolf himself, waiting for Brer Rabbit and his cheeky friends.

And when they came, and began to sing and dance, old Brer Wolf grinned to himself. They thought they were being funny, did they? Well, he'd show them just how funny they were!

Brer Rabbit and Flip and Flop were dancing round hand in

hand—and suddenly the old black scarecrow moved in the moonlight, stretched out a big paw, and then another—and all those three rabbits were caught!

My, my! What a scare they got! Brer Rabbit knew in a trice what had happened, and he kicked himself to think how easily he had been tricked. This was bad, there was no mistake about it. Brer Wolf had the right to be angry, and Brer Rabbit was quite sure he would be.

Brer Wolf took the three rabbits to his house. He stalked along over the fields in the long coat belonging to the scare-crow, looking very queer indeed. He went into his house, took off the coat, flung it on the floor, and glared at the three scared rabbits.

"And now," said Brer Wolf in a horrid sort of voice, "I'm going to put a pot on to boil. I'm just going to show you three rabbits what happens to people who take my turnips."

"Please, Brer Wolf, we're very sorry," said Brer Rabbit in a humble voice. But Brer Wolf didn't listen. He went into his kitchen and shut and locked the door behind him, leaving the three rabbits in the parlour. The window was fastened tightly. There was no escape!

Brer Rabbit sat and listened to the sounds of a pot being filled with water and set on the fire. He trembled and shook. What was he to do? How could he save himself and his cousins? How he wished he had never touched turnips in his life!

He saw the long coat of the scarecrow on the floor and he picked it up. An idea came into his head and he poked Flip and Flop quickly. He whispered to them.

"We'll all get into this coat, and I'll button it up. Flip, get in first, so that your feet show at the bottom. Flop, stand on Flip's shoulders, and I'll button the coat round you. That's right. Now I'll climb in at the top—like this—and stand on Flop's shoulders."

Brer Rabbit was now standing on Flop's shoulders, and he buttoned the coat tightly round his own neck. It looked for all the world as if Brer Rabbit was a giant rabbit! There were rabbit's feet at the bottom and a rabbit's head at the top! Brer Rabbit caught sight of himself in the glass and he grinned.

"Flip, walk to the door," he ordered. Flip went to the door and Brer Rabbit knocked on it hard.

"Brer Wolf! Brer Wolf! Open the door and let me go! If you don't, you'll be sorry for yourself!"

Brer Wolf put the pot on the fire and shouted back:

"The pot's ready! I'm just a-coming!"

Brer Rabbit banged so loudly on the door that Brer Wolf almost upset the pot.

"Brer Wolf! You'll get a shock when you see me! That pot won't be big enough! I'm a giant!"

"Don't talk rubbish," said Brer Wolf crossly. "This pot of mine will cook the lot of you!"

"Brer Wolf, I tell you, you'll get a shock!" said Brer Rabbit, hitting the door with a stool. "Can't you hear how big and strong my fists are, hitting your door like this!"

Brer Wolf was afraid the door would be broken and hurried to open it. He unlocked it—and at once Brer Rabbit walked through, taller than Brer Wolf himself, for Flip and Flop were beneath him, balancing each other, and he was on the top!

"Ooooof!" said Brer Wolf, as scared as could be. "What have you done to yourself, Brer Rabbit?"

"I tell you, I'm a-growing and a-growing!" said Brer Rabbit, grinning. "Brer Wolf, would you like a fight with me? I'm bigger than you are now! No—I'll just wait a few minutes and grow some more, and maybe I'll be strong enough then to pick you up and take you home with me and put you in *my* pot!"

"You go out right now, you go out right now!" cried Brer Wolf in a fright, for he really thought that Brer Rabbit was growing into a giant animal before his eyes. He pushed Brer Rabbit to the door and Brer Rabbit was mighty glad to go! Flip's legs went as fast as possible, carrying Flop and Brer Rabbit above him, and as soon as they reached a bush, the giant rabbit fell to the ground and split into three!

One rabbit went one way, one went another, and Brer Rabbit shot off to his house. He didn't feel really safe till he was in his kitchen, with the door bolted and barred behind him.

"I'll never steal turnips again!" he vowed to himself. "No, I'll never do it again!"

And wasn't Brer Wolf astonished to meet Brer Rabbit the next week, and see that he was his right size again! "I thought you'd grown to a giant!" he said.

"Oh, I grew back again," said Brer Rabbit. "All my clothes were too small, you see. But just you be careful you don't catch me again, Brer Wolf, or I'll grow twice as big as you, and chase you round the woods like a mouse! Ho ho, you just be careful!"

"There's been a trick somewhere!" thought Brer Wolf to himself. "But WHAT WAS IT?"

He'll never know—poor old Brer Wolf!

Brer Fox's Cabbages

Once Brer Fox and Brer Rabbit saved up some money and went to market to buy some cabbages. They spent all their money; and filled their cart with fine fat cabbages.

" Cabbage soup ! " said Brer Rabbit, as he climbed into the cart. Brer Fox shook the reins of the old horse.

" Cabbage broth ! " he said, and licked his lips. The old horse set off at a canter, with Brer Fox driving her, and Brer Rabbit sitting comfortably on the cabbages.

Now they hadn't gone very far before Brer Fox said something that Brer Rabbit didn't like at all !

" I guess we'll be meeting Brer Wolf along here," said Brer Fox in a bright sort of voice. " I guess he'll want a lift too. You won't mind making room for him at the back there, will you, Brer Rabbit ? "

Old Brer Rabbit pricked up his ears. He didn't want Brer Wolf near him at all—Brer Wolf was always far too hungry for Brer Rabbit to feel safe beside him.

" Now, Brer Fox," said Brer Rabbit in a cross voice, " you know I can't bear Brer Wolf. I won't have you giving him a lift when I'm in the cart."

" I don't see how I can stop old Brer Wolf jumping in the cart if he wants to," said Brer Fox, grinning away to himself, for he guessed Brer Rabbit was in a nice fix.

" Well, Brer Fox, if you let Brer Wolf in, I shall jump out ! " said Brer Rabbit in a rage.

" Oh, you jump out if you want to, Brer Rabbit," said Brer Fox. " But I shouldn't be surprised if Brer Wolf keeps your cabbages if you leave them here in the cart."

Brer Rabbit glared at Brer Fox's back. He knew quite well he was being tricked. Brer Fox had taken him to market, had helped him to spend all his money on cabbages, and had planned for Brer Wolf to jump in the cart on the way home and frighten away Brer Rabbit. Then poor Brer Rabbit would lose all his cabbages.

But Brer Rabbit didn't mean to be tricked like that, not he. He gave a loud yell, and the horse stopped so suddenly that Brer Fox nearly fell off the driving-seat.

" What's the matter, Brer Rabbit ? " said Brer Fox crossly. " What do you want to do that for ? "

" Brer Fox ! Can't you hear dogs barking ? " asked Brer Rabbit, putting up his hand to his ear. Brer Fox looked frightened. He was dreadfully afraid of dogs.

" Just wait here a minute and I'll pop into the wood and climb a tree," said Brer Rabbit. " Then I shall be able to see if there are dogs coming after you, Brer Fox."

He scuttled into the wood. Brer Fox waited impatiently, listening hard for the barking of dogs. But he couldn't hear a thing.

Old Brer Rabbit wasn't climbing any trees, not he! He was doing something queer. He was filling his pockets with stones as fast as possible.

Brer Fox grew impatient and shouted out to Brer Rabbit: "Can you see any dogs? Hurry up!"

"Oh, Brer Fox! Oh, Brer Fox!" cried Brer Rabbit, running out, and panting as if he had been climbing up and down a tall tree. "There's hundreds of dogs! Horrid dogs! And they've smelt you, and they're coming along the woodland road as fast as can be, their tongues hanging out! They're coming so fast that they haven't even time to bark now!"

"Get in, get in, Brer Rabbit!" shouted Brer Fox in a terrible fright. "I'll have to drive at top-speed. You shout at the dogs and keep them off if they catch up to us!"

"But how shall I keep them off?" said Brer Rabbit. "There's only our cabbages to throw at them."

"Well, throw those, then, throw those!" yelled Brer Fox,

and he whipped the horse, who began to gallop down the woodland road so fast that the cart bumped and swayed in a most dangerous manner.

The cart and the horse made a great noise, and when Brer Rabbit began to shout too, Brer Fox felt sure the dogs were near and were barking, but he couldn't hear them because of all the noise. He whipped the horse still faster.

Then Brer Rabbit began to throw out the big stones he had collected, pretending to throw them at the dogs who weren't there! Plonk! Plonk! Thud!

"There goes a cabbage!" shouted Brer Rabbit, though it was only a stone. "It hit that dog on the nose! Here goes another cabbage! It's hit a dog too! Go away, you wicked creatures! I'll throw cabbages at you till you're green!"

Brer Fox went on whipping up the horse, and called to Brer Rabbit to fling out more cabbages to keep the dogs off. Brer Rabbit was having a high old time, yelling and dancing about on the cabbages, and flinging out stones for all he was worth.

Presently they came to where old Brer Wolf was waiting for his lift, his face one big grin. Brer Fox saw him, but he didn't stop. The horse went galloping past, and Brer Rabbit aimed an extra big stone at the surprised Brer Wolf. It hit him on the snout.

"The dogs are after us, Brer Wolf! The dogs!" yelled Brer Fox, as he thundered by.

Brer Wolf couldn't see any dogs at all. He was most astonished. He thought Brer Fox had gone quite mad. He rubbed his nose where the stone had hit him, and went home again, feeling very angry.

"Brer Fox, Brer Fox, the dogs will have you in a minute!" cried Brer Rabbit, when they were safely past Brer Wolf. "You'd better jump for it when you come to that old hollow tree. You'll be safe in there. You jump for that tree, Brer Fox!"

So when he came to the hollow tree, Brer Fox jumped for it. He gave a frightened look behind to see the dogs, but he couldn't seem to see any. He disappeared inside the hollow tree, and stayed there, trembling like a jelly.

"Good-bye, Brer Fox, good-bye!" cried Brer Rabbit, climbing into the driver's seat and shaking the reins. "See you to-morrow!"

He cantered off home at a good pace. When he got there, he grinned to see what a fine load of green cabbages he had. He wasn't going to take any to Brer Fox's! No! Brer Fox had meant to rob him of his share—and now old Brer Fox was going without *his*!

Brer Rabbit filled his larder from top to toe with green cabbages. "Cabbage soup!" he said, rubbing his hands in glee. "Cabbage broth! Pickled cabbage! Cabbage salad! My, there's enough to keep me happy till Christmas!"

The next day Brer Fox came calling round at Brer Rabbit's for his horse and cart.

"So the dogs didn't get you after all!" said Brer Rabbit, pretending to be surprised. "There's your horse and cart, Brer Fox. Sorry about the cabbages."

"Did you throw them *all* at those dogs you said were following us?" said Brer Fox, sniffing the air.

"Well, Brer Fox, you can see there are no cabbages in the cart," said Brer Rabbit.

"Yes, Brer Rabbit, I can see that," said Brer Fox, looking angry. "But I can smell CABBAGE SOUP!"

"Dear me, *I* can't help what you smell!" said Brer Rabbit with a laugh, and he slammed his door and bolted it. And Brer Fox had to go without his cabbages that winter. Wasn't he angry!

Poor Old Brer Bear

ONCE IT happened that Brer Rabbit was chased so hard by Brer Fox that he just had to climb up a tree. Now this was mighty difficult for him, and he wouldn't have done it at all if there had been a hole near, but there wasn't

So up he scrabbled, panting and puffing, and sat up on a high branch, looking down at Brer Fox. Brer Fox wasn't good at climbing trees, so he sat at the foot of the tree and scowled.

"Come on down, Brer Rabbit," he said, "come on down."

"I can't," said Brer Rabbit. "It was difficult enough to get up—but I'm mighty certain I'd break my neck if I jumped down."

Brer Fox looked up at the high branch on which Brer Rabbit sat, and he knew that Brer Rabbit spoke the truth. He couldn't get down!

"Well, I'm a-going to get my axe, Brer Rabbit," said Brer Fox. "I'm going to chop down this tree and get you this time! You can just stay there till I come back! Then down you'll come with the tree, smack!"

Brer Fox ran off. Brer Rabbit sat up in the tree, looking blue. Should he drop down and hope he wouldn't be hurt? Should he stay where he was and hope to escape when the tree came down? He looked down at the ground. No—it was too far away, that was certain.

Just then Brer Rabbit heard the sound of some one lumbering through the wood, singing a deep, growly song.

"That's Brer Bear," thought Brer Rabbit, peering through the leaves. And then Brer Rabbit sat back on his branch and began to laugh loudly. My, how he laughed!

"Ho ho ho!" he roared. "Ha ha ha! What a funny sight! Ha ha ha!"

Brer Bear heard the laughter, and he stopped in surprise. He looked in front of him. He looked behind him. He looked each side of him. But he couldn't see anyone laughing at all. Still the sound went on and on.

"Ho ho ho ho! Ha ha ha ha!"

Then Brer Bear looked up, and he saw old Brer Rabbit sitting on the branch laughing so much that he could hardly hold on.

Every now and again Brer Rabbit would look through the leaves as if he were watching something, and then he would lean back, open his mouth and laugh and laugh.

Brer Bear watched him. He felt very curious to know what Brer Rabbit was laughing at. It must be something he was peeping at through the leaves.

At last Brer Bear could stand it no longer. He called up to Brer Rabbit:

"Heyo, Brer Rabbit! What's the matter up there? What's the joke?"

At first Brer Rabbit took no notice of Brer Bear at all, but just went on peeping through the leaves and roaring with laughter.

Brer Bear got angry and shouted at him:

"Brer Rabbit! What's the joke? What are you laughing at?"

Brer Rabbit looked down at Brer Bear. "Heyo, Brer Bear!" he said. "Go away, please. I'm just enjoying myself up here."

"I can see you are," said Brer Bear crossly. "But please tell me the joke."

"Well, Brer Bear, from here I can see old Mr. Benjamin Ram playing his fiddle," said Brer Rabbit, quite untruthfully. "And he's teaching old Mrs. Benjamin Ram to dance, and his two children too—and you can't imagine how funny they all look, treading on one another's toes!"

Brer Bear wanted to see them too. So he tried to climb the tree, but it was too high even for him.

"If you want to come up and see, you must get a ladder, Brer Bear," said Brer Rabbit. "Hurry up, now, because maybe the dancing-class will soon be over!"

Brer Bear lumbered away to his house, which was just nearby, and fetched a ladder. He put it against the tree and climbed up to Brer Rabbit's branch.

"Now where's this funny dancing-class?" he said, and peered through the leaves. "I can't see a thing yet."

"Come in my place," said Brer Rabbit, spying old Brer Fox coming along in the distance with an axe. "I'll slip down the ladder and give you room, Brer Bear."

So Brer Rabbit slid off the branch and gave Brer Bear his place. He slipped down that ladder at top speed, put it on his shoulder, and was away through the bushes before old Brer Fox came along with his axe.

Brer Bear sat up in the tree, grumbling away because he couldn't see Mr. Benjamin Ram teaching his family to dance. Brer Fox came up, set his axe to the tree-trunk, and began to chop.

Brer Bear heard the noise and looked down.

"Hey, Brer Fox! What are you doing down there?" he called in alarm.

Brer Fox looked up in surprise. He couldn't believe his eyes when he saw Brer Bear up there instead of Brer Rabbit.

"Tails and whiskers!" he cried. "I leave Brer Rabbit on that branch and I come back and find Brer Bear. What are *you* doing up there?"

"I'm trying to see Mr. Benjamin Ram giving his family a dancing-lesson," said Brer Bear. "I'm told it's a mighty funny sight."

"But how did you get up the tree?" asked Brer Fox, still surprised.

"Up the ladder, of course, silly," said Brer Bear, thinking that Brer Fox was quite mad. He didn't know that Brer Rabbit had gone, and had taken the ladder with him.

"What ladder?" asked Brer Fox, thinking in his turn that Brer Bear was also quite mad.

"*My* ladder!" roared Brer Bear. "Can't you see it?"

"No," said Brer Fox. "Where's Brer Rabbit, Brer Bear? Is he up there with you?"

"He was, just now," said Brer Bear, looking around him in the tree. "Maybe he's slipped down the ladder."

Brer Fox gave a shout of anger. "That's just what he *has* done, Brer Bear—*and* taken the ladder with him too! What did you want to go and bring a ladder for, just when I'd got Brer Rabbit nicely caught up in the tree?"

Brer Bear stared in surprise. "How was *I* to know that you'd got him caught?" he asked. "When I came along, old Brer Rabbit was laughing fit to kill himself, because he said he could see Mr. Benjamin Ram teaching his family to dance. So I got a ladder and came up to see too. But I haven't seen a thing yet."

"No, and you never will," said Brer Fox, putting his axe on his shoulder. "But you can stay there all day and look, if you like, you silly, stupid, brainless creature!"

"Hie! Don't you say things like that to me!" said Brer Bear in a rage. "And just you fetch me a ladder, Brer Fox, for I can't get down here without one. I'm not going to stay here all day looking at something that isn't there."

"Oh, but you'll have to," said Brer Fox spitefully. And he was right. Brer Bear did have to. He couldn't get down till Mrs. Bear brought him another ladder that evening. As for Brer Rabbit, he laughed till the tears ran down his whiskers, whenever he thought of old Brer Fox and Brer Bear.

Brer Fox and the Pimmerly Plum

ONE TIME when the sun was mighty hot, old Brer Terrapin was going down the road. He went on and on and he felt mighty tired. He puffed and he blew and he panted, just the same old Creepumcrawlum. He went on down the high road and came to the stream.

He crawled into the water and took a drink, and then he crawled out the other side, and sat down under the shade of a tree. When he had got back his breath, he looked up at the sun to see what time of day it was—and then he saw that he was sitting in the shade of a big plane-tree.

> " *Good luck to them, good luck again*
> *That sit in the shade of the great big plane !* "

sang Brer Terrapin.

Well, Brer Terrapin felt so nice and cool that it wasn't long before he began to nod, and by and by he dropped off into a sound sleep. Of course, Brer Terrapin carried his house with him wherever he went, so all he had to do when he slept was to shut his door and there he was as snug as the old black cat under the barn !

Brer Terrapin lay there, he did, and slept and slept. He didn't know how long he'd been asleep, but suddenly he felt that somebody was playing about with him. He kept his door shut and lay there and listened. He felt somebody turning him and his shelly-house round and round and round.

This scared Brer Terrapin, because he knew that if his house was turned upside down he would find it very hard to get right way up again. So he opened his door a little way and peeped out, and he saw Brer Fox playing about with him. Then Brer Terrapin opened his door a little farther, he did, and began to laugh as loudly as a horse.

"Well, well, well! Who'd have thought it! Old Brer Fox, smart as you like, has come to catch me! And he comes at a good time, too! I'm so full that I can hardly see straight. I've been eating Pimmerly Plums all the morning!"

Now, in these days, the Pimmerly Plum was very scarce, and only Brer Rabbit and Brer Terrapin had ever seen it or tasted it. It was a most delicious plum, round and full of sweet juice that just tripped down the throat. So, when Brer Fox heard Brer Terrapin talking about the Pimmerly Plum, he cocked up his ears and listened, and let Brer Terrapin alone. Brer Terrapin laughed and laughed, and Brer Fox couldn't make out why.

"Hush, Brer Terrapin! You make my mouth water with your talk of the Pimmerly Plum. You just tell me whereabouts I can find that plum, and I'll let you alone."

Well, Brer Terrapin laughed again, and then he cleared his throat and sang:

"*A pound of sugar and a pound of gum*
Isn't so sweet as the Pimmerly Plum!"

Brer Fox lifted up his hands and shouted: "Oh, hush, Brer Terrapin! You just make my mouth water! Whereabouts is that Pimmerly Plum?"

"You're standing right under the tree, Brer Fox! That's what makes me laugh! You're standing right under the tree, and you don't know it!"

"Brer Terrapin, surely not?"

"Yes, there you stand, Brer Fox!"

Brer Fox looked up into the plane-tree and he was astonished —for all over the tree grew little round balls—the balls of the plane-tree. Brer Fox thought they were the Pimmerly Plums, sure enough, especially as Brer Terrapin kept on and on telling him they were.

"How am I going to get those Pimmerly Plums?" said Brer Fox. "This is a mighty big tree—and though I can beat you at climbing, Brer Terrapin, I don't see how I can get up that tree, indeed I don't."

Brer Terrapin, he just laughed, and said nothing. Brer Fox went on looking up into the plane-tree, thinking hard.

"I see those Pimmerly Plums hanging there, so small and round, Brer Terrapin," said Brer Fox, "but how am I going to get them?"

Then Brer Terrapin opened his door a little way and shouted:

"Ah-yi! That's where an old Slickum-Slow-come like me knows best! You're mighty smart, Brer Fox, but somehow or other you're not so smart as old Slickum-Slow-come!"

"Now, Brer Terrapin," said Brer Fox, "how in the name of goodness do you get those plums?"

"I'm not going to tell you, Brer Fox. You haven't got time to get them, so where's the use of me telling you?"

"Brer Terrapin, I can take a week to get them."

"Well, if I tell you how to get them, you'll go round telling all the other creatures, and then that will be the last of the Pimmerly Plum, Brer Fox."

"Brer Terrapin, I won't tell anyone. Just try me and see."

Brer Terrapin pretended to think for a little while. Then he said: "I'll tell you, then, Brer Fox. When I want a Pimmerly Plum, I just come to this tree, and I get right under it, just as you see me now. Then I throw back my head and open my mouth. I open my mouth, and when the Pimmerly Plum drops, it drops right into my mouth—spang! All you've got to do is to sit and wait, Brer Fox."

Brer Fox listened and said nothing. He just sat down under the tree, he did, threw back his head and opened his mouth. He looked very strange, sitting there like that, quite still, with his mouth wide open, waiting for a plum to drop into it.

Well, he sat there, and he sat there, with his mouth open, and every time Brer Terrapin looked at him it was as much as the old Shellyback could do to keep from bursting out laughing. But by and by he took his way towards home, Brer Terrapin did, chuckling and laughing, and it wasn't long before he met old Brer Rabbit lolloping along down the road. Brer Rabbit saw Brer Terrapin laughing and he called to him:

"What's tickling you so, Brer Terrapin?"

"Oh, Brer Rabbit," said Brer Terrapin. "I'm so tickled I can hardly shuffle along. There's old Brer Fox sitting along

there under the plane-tree, a-waiting for a Pimmerly Plum to drop into his mouth!"

And Brer Terrapin told Brer Rabbit the whole story. Brer Rabbit listened and grinned and grinned and listened.

He loped off and watched Brer Fox sitting there with his head flung back and his mouth wide open—and it wasn't long before Brer Rabbit gathered a few stones together and threw them gently at Brer Fox's mouth.

My! Brer Fox thought they were the Pimmerly Plums dropping in all right, and he swallowed and swallowed every time a stone came in! And goodness knows how many stones he would have eaten, if he hadn't heard old Brer Rabbit laughing fit to kill himself!

If anyone wanted to get Brer Fox into a temper after that he just had to ask him one question: "Have you been eating any more Pimmerly Plums, Brer Fox?" And then I promise you they would see Brer Fox snapping his jaws and looking mighty red about the eyes!

Brer Rabbit is Very Kind

ONCE BRER BEAR got very tired of Brer Rabbit, and he made up his mind to get him, if it took him a month of Sundays to do it.

"I'll just go round and follow him everywhere," thought Brer Bear to himself. "Sooner or later I'll surprise him and get him all right. Then that will be the end of his tricks."

So Brer Bear began to follow Brer Rabbit around all day and every day. Brer Rabbit thought it was funny at first, and he took Brer Bear a lot of long walks till Brer Bear was tired out.

But Brer Rabbit was tired out too, so he soon gave that up. He got very angry with Brer Bear. If he went into his garden, there was Brer Bear standing by the gate. If he went to walk in the woods, Brer Bear was sure to be hiding behind a tree. If he went to get water from the well, Brer Bear would be sitting the other side, waiting to catch him.

"This is making me feel scared," said Brer Rabbit to himself at last. "I can't keep looking out for Brer Bear every minute of the day and night. Maybe he'll give up. He'll get tired of it."

But once Brer Bear had made up his mind to anything, there was no stopping him, and no tiring him. He just went on and on and on. It was most annoying.

And then Brer Rabbit began to think. He sat down and he thought and thought how he might make things better for himself. Then he jumped up, slapped his knee, and capered off to the town to buy something.

Brer Bear lumbered after him, but Brer Rabbit got there a

long way first. He went to a shop that sold watches and he asked to see some. He put each watch to his ear and listened to it.

"I want the one with the very loudest tick," he said.

"Well, most people want a quiet watch," said the shopman. "But I've got an old watch that has a tick like a grandfather clock! Maybe that would suit you!"

He brought out a big old watch whose tick was certainly very loud indeed! Brer Rabbit was pleased. He bought the watch and then set off to the post-office with it. He posted it to Brer Bear with a note inside.

The note said:

"DEAR BRER BEAR,—I'm mighty glad you are following Brer Rabbit about. Here's a reward for your patience. Please wear it, with best wishes from

"COUSIN WILDCAT."

Brer Bear was surprised and delighted with the letter and the watch. "Dear me," he said, putting the watch into his pocket, "I'd no idea Cousin Wildcat knew what I was doing. What a generous creature he is! I'll ask him in to dinner when I've got Brer Rabbit at last."

And now Brer Rabbit didn't need to keep a look-out for Brer Bear everywhere, because as soon as he came anywhere near him, he always heard the same warning sound:

"TICK, TOCK, TICK, TOCK!"

Then Brer Rabbit would shout out loudly, "Heyo, Brer Bear! I can see you! Peep-bo!"

And Brer Bear would be most astonished, especially if he was hiding right inside a bush or down a hole. It didn't seem to matter where he hid, Brer Rabbit always seemed to see him and shout loudly, "Heyo, Brer Bear! I can see you! Peep-bo!"

Brer Bear hid up a tree, and the leaves were thick around him. But as soon as Brer Rabbit came along that way he pricked up his ears and heard "TICK, TOCK, TICK, TOCK!" from Brer Bear's big new watch. Then he would stop and cry, "Peep-bo! Peep-bo! I can see you, Brer Bear! It's no good trying to hide from *me!*"

Brer Bear once hid himself under a great rock, and he knew Brer Rabbit couldn't possibly see him. But that wasn't a bit of good either, for as soon as Brer Rabbit came pattering by, he stopped and shouted, "Oh, so you're there, are you, Brer Bear! Playing peep-bo again! What a funny fellow you are!"

Brer Bear gave it up after a week or two, and Brer Fox asked him why.

"Oh, Brer Rabbit has got eyes like a hundred eagles!" said Brer Bear in disgust. "He can see through trees and walls and rocks! It's just no good at all, Brer Fox."

"Well, let me hide the other side of this thick wall with you, Brer Bear," said Brer Fox.

"I guess he can't really see through that!"

So the two of them sat down and hid—and presently along came Brer Rabbit, lippitty, clippitty, lippitty, clippitty, as usual. And he heard the sound of Brer Bear's watch again, "TICK, TOCK, TICK, TOCK, TICK, TOCK!"

He saw the print of Brer Fox's feet too, and he grinned. "So Brer Fox is there too!" he said to himself. "Well, he won't be there long!"

He went to the nearby well and filled the bucket with water. He carried it to the wall—and, slishy-slosh, all the water poured down on to the heads of the alarmed Brer Bear and Brer Fox!

"Peep-bo, Brer Bear! Peep-bo, Brer Fox!" cried Brer Rabbit, standing on the top of the wall. "Did you think I couldn't see through the wall? Oh yes, I can—and I saw you both sitting there, as snug as can be! This is a fine game you're playing—but I shall always win it!"

Brer Fox sprang away and Brer Bear lumbered after him. "What's the good of hiding and waiting for a person that has got eyes like that?" grumbled Brer Bear.

"No good at all!" said Brer Fox, and he shook the water from his coat. "Just leave him alone, Brer Bear. That's the best thing to do with Brer Rabbit."

And you may be sure that Brer Rabbit quite agreed!

Brer Bear's Honey-Pots

SOMEONE had been stealing Brer Bear's honey-pots. It wasn't Brer Rabbit, for he didn't know where Brer Bear kept them that year. Brer Bear just simply didn't know *who* it was! He told Brer Rabbit all about it when they met.

"Well," said Brer Rabbit, "what about giving *me* the pots to keep for you, Brer Bear? They'll be safe then."

"Huh!" said Brer Bear scornfully. "Yes—just as safe as a bird in a cat's mouth. I don't trust you, Brer Rabbit, and I never did."

"Brer Bear, you make me angry," said Brer Rabbit. "If I said I'd keep those honey-pots for you safely, I'd keep them. But now I've a good mind to take them away from you just to punish you!"

"I shan't tell you where I hide them," said Brer Bear.

The snow began to fall thickly just then, and Brer Rabbit put up his coat-collar. The snow was already deep on the ground, and every tree and bush wore a white nightcap.

"The safest place to hide your honey-pots would be somewhere under the snow!" shouted Brer Rabbit as he trudged off home.

Well, Brer Bear thought about that—and the more he thought about it, the more he thought it was a good idea.

So he went to get what was left of his pots of honey, and he fetched a spade too. He dug a fine deep place in the snow, and he buried three pots there—then he dug another hole and buried three more pots in the snow—and after that he dug a third place, and put the last three pots there.

He patted the snow down over them. "That's good!" he said to himself. "Now no one will steal my honey-pots—and even if they find *one* of the hiding-places, they won't find them all." And off went old Brer Bear, as pleased as could be.

Brer Rabbit didn't go to bed that night. He knew quite well that the wind had changed and was blowing from the warm south. The snow was going to melt!

The moon peeped out from behind the clouds every now and again. Brer Rabbit pricked up his ears and listened to a little noise that had suddenly began.

"That's the snow melting on my roof and running down in drips!" said Brer Rabbit. "I can hear it. I'll stay up a bit longer and see if the snow will melt to-night."

So he stayed up a bit longer, and sure enough all the snow everywhere began to melt. It ran away into water, and except in the very coldest places there was no snow to be seen just before dawn.

Brer Rabbit lighted his lantern. He took a basket. He set out in the dark, splashing through the wet lanes. The moon had disappeared behind thick clouds now, so he was glad of his lantern-light.

When he came to Brer Bear's house, he lifted up his lantern and shone it on Brer Bear's garden which had been deep in snow when Brer Rabbit had left it earlier in the evening. Now nearly all the snow had gone—and in three places there were little mounds of honey-pots!

Brer Rabbit grinned. He picked up the honey and put the nine pots into his basket. Then he set off for home again, splashing through the puddles that had been left by the melted snow.

And when Brer Bear looked out in the morning, what a shock he got! The snow was gone—and his honey-pots were gone too! He rushed out into the garden in a tremendous rage.

"They're gone! They're gone!" he shouted.

Brer Rabbit was just passing, and he looked most surprised. "What are gone?" he asked.

"My honey-pots!" cried Brer Bear, dancing about in rage. "I hid them in the snow—and the snow melted, and I don't know where my honey-pots have gone!"

"Perhaps they've melted too," said Brer Rabbit.

"Don't be silly," said Brer Bear in a rage. "Oh, I'd give anything to know where my last nine pots of honey are!"

"What would you give?" asked Brer Rabbit.

"I'd give my new blue scarf," said Brer Bear. Then he stared at Brer Rabbit. "Do *you* know where they are?" he asked.

"Oh yes," said Brer Rabbit. "Bring your new blue scarf, Brer Bear, and I'll show you where your honey is."

Brer Bear fetched his lovely blue scarf. Brer Rabbit took him to his house—and there, on his larder shelf, were the nine pots of honey. "You can take them," he said to Brer Bear. "I told you they would be safe if *I* kept them for you. But give me your blue scarf, Brer Bear."

Brer Bear scowled. He gave Brer Rabbit the scarf. He took the nine pots of honey and stepped out of the door.

"You're a wicked rabbit," he said. "I believe you *knew* the snow was going to melt last night."

"'Course I knew," said Brer Rabbit. "Didn't the wind

change just as I was talking to you last night? If you weren't so stupid, Brer Bear, you'd have noticed it too. Well—thanks for the scarf!"

And old Brer Rabbit tied it round his neck in a beautiful bow. He wore it whenever he went to call on Brer Bear, which was very annoying and tiresome of him. But you simply can't do *any*thing with old Brer Rabbit!

Brer Fox is Too Smart

One day when Brer Fox went calling on Miss Meadows and the girls, who should he find sitting up there but old Brer Rabbit? There he was, just as cheeky as you please! He was teasing the girls and making them giggle, and nobody seemed very pleased to see old Brer Fox.

"You must excuse us for making such a gigglement, Brer Fox," said Miss Meadows, "but Brer Rabbit does say such funny things!"

Brer Fox felt sure that the funny things Brer Rabbit had been saying were all about *him*. But he joined in the fun, and soon he was feeling all splimmy-splammy. All the same, he kept his eye on Brer Rabbit, and Brer Rabbit soon began to feel it would be better for him to leave before Brer Fox did.

So after a while Brer Rabbit looked out towards the sunset and said: "Now then, folks and friends, I must say good-bye. Clouds are coming up yonder, and before we know it, the rain will be pouring and the grass will be growing!"

Well, Brer Fox looked out too, and said: "Yes, the clouds are coming up, and I expect I'd better be getting along myself, Miss Meadows. I don't want to get my best Sunday-go-to-meeting clothes wet."

Miss Meadows and the girls begged them to stay, but they had both made up their minds to go, and after a while they set out.

Well, whilst they were going down the big road, talking to one another, and Brer Rabbit was a-wondering how he could get rid of Brer Fox, Brer Fox suddenly stopped right in the road and said:

" Run, run, Brer Rabbit! Look here! There are Mr. Dog's tracks and, what's more, they are just freshly made!"

Brer Rabbit sidled up to look. " Huh!" he said, " that footprint would never fit Mr. Dog's foot! And what's more, Brer Fox, I know who made that track, and I knew him long, long ago!"

" Tell me his name, Brer Rabbit," begged Brer Fox.

Brer Rabbit laughed. " If I'm not mistaken, Brer Fox, the poor creature that made that track is Cousin Wildcat, for sure."

" How big is he, Brer Rabbit?" asked Brer Fox, still scared.

" Oh, he's just about your height, Brer Fox," said Brer Rabbit. Then Brer Rabbit pretended to be talking to himself. " Tut, tut, tut! It's mighty funny I should come across Cousin Wildcat in this part of the world. To be sure, to be sure! Many's the time I saw my old grand-daddy kick and cuff Cousin Wildcat till I felt really sorry for him. If you want any fun, Brer Fox, right now is the time to get it!"

" How am I going to have any fun with Cousin Wildcat?" said Brer Fox.

" Easy enough," said Brer Rabbit. " Just go after old Cousin Wildcat, run at him and lam him round!"

Brer Fox scratched his ear and said: " Brer Rabbit, I'm afraid. His footprint is too much like Mr. Dog's."

Brer Rabbit sat right down in the road and shouted and laughed. " Shoo, Brer Fox!" he said. " Who'd have thought you'd be so frightened? Just come and look at this track closely. Can you see the mark of any claws anywhere?"

Well, Brer Fox looked—and as cats always draw in their claws when they go walking, of course Cousin Wildcat hadn't left any sign of his at all. And Brer Fox nodded his head and said: " Yes, you're right, Brer Rabbit. There is no sign of any claws there."

"Well, then," said Brer Rabbit, "if he hasn't got any claws, how can he hurt you?"

"What about his teeth, Brer Rabbit?" said Brer Fox.

"Shoo, Brer Fox! Creatures that gnaw the bark of trees, won't bite *you*!"

Well, Brer Fox took another good look at the tracks, and then he and Brer Rabbit set out to follow them. They went down the lane and across the turnip-patch, and down a drain and up a big ditch. Brer Rabbit did the tracking, and every time he saw a footprint he shouted:

"Here's another track, and no claw there! Here's another track, and no claw there!"

They kept on and they kept on, till by and by they came up to the creature himself—Cousin Wildcat. Brer Rabbit shouted out in a mighty biggitty voice: "Heyo there! What are you doing?"

The creature looked round but he didn't say a word. "Huh!" said Brer Rabbit, "you needn't look so sulky! We'll make you talk before we've done with you. Come now! What are you doing here?"

The wildcat rubbed himself against a tree just like a house-cat rubs himself against a chair, but he didn't say a word. Brer Rabbit went on shouting.

"What have you come pestering us for? We haven't been pestering you! You may think I don't know who you are, but I do. You're the same Cousin Wildcat that my grand-daddy used to kick and cuff when you wouldn't answer. I'll just tell you I've got a better man here than my grand-daddy ever was, and I promise you he'll make you talk!"

The wildcat leaned harder against the tree, and his eyes gleamed, and he ruffled up and bristled, but still he didn't say a word. Brer Rabbit didn't go a step nearer—no, he was leaving all that to Brer Fox—but he turned to Brer Fox and

said: " Go on, Brer Fox, and if he won't answer you, slap him down. That's the way my grand-daddy did. You go on, Brer Fox, and if he dares to try and run, I'll just whirl in and catch him for you."

Well, Brer Fox was sort of doubtful, but he started off towards the wildcat. Old Cousin Wildcat walked all round the tree, rubbing himself, but he didn't say a word. Brer Rabbit shouted out: " Just walk right up and give him a slap, Brer Fox! The sulky rogue! Just smack him on the nose, and if he runs, I'll catch him!"

Brer Fox went up a little nearer. Cousin Wildcat stopped rubbing on the tree and sat up on his hind legs with his front paws in the air, balancing himself by leaning against the tree—but he didn't say a word.

Brer Rabbit squalled out: " Oh, you needn't put your

hands up and try and beg for mercy! That's the way you tricked my old grand-daddy, but you can't trick me! All your sitting up and begging won't help you! If you're as humble as all that, why don't you answer when we speak to you? Give him a slap, Brer Fox! If he runs, I'll catch him."

Well, Brer Fox looked at the wildcat sitting there looking so humble as if he were begging for mercy, and he grinned at Brer Rabbit. He sidled up towards the creature, and put up his paw to slap him—but just as he raised his paw old Cousin Wildcat drew back and hit Brer Fox a blow across his nose—with all his claws out!

Brer Rabbit knew quite well this would happen. He heard Brer Fox squalling as if the sky had fallen on top of him! As for Cousin Wildcat, he glared at Brer Fox as if he would tear him in two. Brer Rabbit danced round in glee and yelled: "Slap him again, Brer Fox! Slap him again! I guess you'll win, Brer Fox! If he runs my way I'll give him such a smack he'll roll a mile! Slap him again!"

All the time that Brer Rabbit was shouting this, poor Brer Fox was sitting down holding his nose with both hands and moaning and groaning: "I'm killed, Brer Rabbit! I'm killed! Run and fetch the doctor! I'm quite killed!"

Cousin Wildcat took a look at Brer Fox, turned away and walked slowly off. Then Brer Rabbit went near and pretended to be most astonished that Brer Fox was hurt. He looked at Brer Fox's nose and said: "Well, well, well, Brer Fox, that wicked creature must have hit you with a handful of nails!"

And with that Brer Rabbit set off for home, and when he got out of sight he sat down and shook with laughter—and it was a mighty good thing for him that Cousin Wildcat wasn't anywhere about, for Brer Rabbit was so weak with laughing that Cousin Wildcat could have made mincemeat of him—no doubt about that!

Brer Rabbit is So Clever

NOW ONCE old Brer Rabbit had a fine store of jam in the barn, that Mrs. Rabbit had made. There wasn't room to put it in the larder, so Brer Rabbit made some shelves in his little barn and put the jam there.

But old Brer Bear soon sniffed it out and he went one night to take some. He got in through the window and went off with seven pots of fine strawberry jam. Brer Rabbit was so angry next day when he found the seven pots missing.

"I'll catch Brer Bear and make him pay dearly for that jam!" said Brer Rabbit to himself. So he went off to find some straw, and put it down in the barn. Then he went to the holly tree and looked under it for some sharp-pointed fallen leaves.

Brer Rabbit mixed the sharp holly leaves in with the straw, grinning away to himself all the time. Now whoever came stealing at night would tread on a prickly leaf and get a shock!

Well, that night along came old Brer Bear for a few more pots of jam again. He climbed in through the window and went to the shelf of jam—and on the way he trod heavily on a sharp-pointed holly leaf! He let out a yell and hopped round in pain.

Brer Rabbit was outside, waiting. He opened the door and rushed in with a big stick. He pretended not to know that Brer Bear was there and he slashed about in the straw as if he was mad!

"I'll get that snake!" he shouted, as he slashed about. "I'll get that snake! It won't bite me if I know anything about it! I'll get that snake!"

Well, when Brer Bear heard Brer Rabbit shouting about a

snake he got very frightened. Was it a snake that had bitten his foot? Oh my, oh my, he might be poisoned and die!

Brer Bear let out a groan and Brer Rabbit stopped slashing about and spoke as if he was mighty surprised.

"Who's there?" he asked.

"It's me—Brer Bear," said Brer Bear, lumbering over to Brer Rabbit in the darkness. "Oh, Brer Rabbit, I think that snake's bitten me!"

He trod on another holly leaf and let out such a yell that he made Brer Rabbit jump. "It's bitten me again!" he shouted. "It's bitten me again! Oh, Brer Rabbit, I'll die! I've been bitten twice by a poisonous snake in the straw."

"Well," said Brer Rabbit, most severely, "I should like to know what you are doing stamping about in my straw at this time of night, Brer Bear."

"Oh, Brer Rabbit, this is no time for asking silly questions," groaned Brer Bear, holding first one foot and then another. "I'm bitten, I tell you. Fetch a doctor."

"Well, first please tell me what you were doing in my barn?" said Brer Rabbit fiercely.

"Oh, Brer Rabbit, if you must know, I was after your

jam," groaned Brer Bear. "And now, please go and get a doctor. Do you want me to die of snake-bite in your barn?"

"Well, it might serve you right," said Brer Rabbit, grinning away to himself in the dark, thinking of the holly leaves in the straw.

Brer Bear tried to get to the door, but unluckily he trod on yet another holly leaf. He gave such a yell that the windows shook!

"That snake's bitten me again! Oh, oh, what shall I do? Go fetch a doctor quickly, Brer Rabbit! You can have back your seven pots of jam!"

"And what else?" demanded Brer Rabbit.

"Oh, you can have seven pots of honey, too," wept Brer Bear.

"Anything else?" asked Brer Rabbit.

"Yes—you can have seven pots of tomato chutney," groaned Brer Bear. Brer Rabbit licked his lips. Mrs. Bear's tomato chutney was simply delicious!

"Well, I'll go and get it all now," said Brer Rabbit. "Now you stay here, Brer Bear, because if you go stamping about the barn that snake is sure to bite you again!"

Off sped Brer Rabbit. He came to Brer Bear's house and got the jam, the honey, and the chutney. He tore back again and set it neatly on the shelf. Brer Bear was lying groaning in the straw, not daring to move.

"I think my legs are swelling up," he said feebly. "I think I'm poisoned all over."

"Well, I'll put some wonderful snake-ointment on you," said Brer Rabbit, grinning away in the darkness. "It will soon make you right!"

Brer Rabbit went into his house and got a tin of black boot-polish. He went to the barn with a lantern.

"Oh, Brer Rabbit, you are kind," said Brer Bear. "Just rub the ointment on and I can go to the doctor then. Rub it on quickly."

Brer Rabbit smeared black boot-polish all over Brer Bear's feet. It smelt horrid.

"There!" he said. "You will find that your feet won't hurt you at all to-morrow. This is wonderful for snake-bites.

Brer Bear cheered up and began to feel better at once. He stood up—and trod on yet another holly leaf! He sat down with a groan. "There must be heaps of snakes here," he said. "Put some more ointment on, Brer Rabbit!"

So old Brer Rabbit rubbed more black boot-polish on, grinning away. "Now, Brer Bear, just you listen to me," he said. "As soon as you get home, lick off all this ointment and put a fresh lot on out of the tin. Don't forget, will you? If you do that, you won't need to go to the doctor."

"Oh, thank you, Brer Rabbit," said Brer Bear gratefully. He hobbled out of the barn, and did not tread on any more holly leaves! Off he went home, glad to find that his legs didn't hurt him at all.

"That must be wonderful ointment Brer Rabbit gave me!" he said to himself. "I will lick it off and put on some more as soon as I get home."

So he sat down when he got home and began to lick off the black boot-polish. It tasted simply terrible. Brer Bear didn't know how he was going to lick it all off. He sat with his tongue hanging out, feeling mighty sick. Then he began licking again—but he just *had* to stop, for the taste was dreadful.

"I'll put the fresh ointment on top of the old," he said at last, and picked up the tin. On it he read, "Black boot-polish!" Brer Bear stared as if he simply couldn't believe his eyes!

"*Boot*-polish! And I've been licking it! *Boot*-polish!" shouted Brer Bear, and he went to rinse out his mouth. But he couldn't get the black off his tongue!

And for two whole weeks, whenever Brer Rabbit met Brer Bear he shouted out, "How's your tongue, Brer Bear? How's your tongue? Let's have a look at your tongue!"

Didn't Brer Bear growl! He'd lost seven pots of honey and seven pots of chutney—and got his tongue well blacked! Poor Brer Bear—he won't go stealing from old Brer Rabbit again!

Brer Rabbit and the Pies

NOW ONCE it happened that Brer Wolf and Brer Fox were going along through the wood to fish in the stream. They carried their lunch with them—and it was meat-pies just baked that morning. They smelt mighty good, and old Brer Rabbit, who was hopping along through the wood at that moment, soon smelt them on the wind.

" Pies ! " said Brer Rabbit. " *Meat*-pies ! Now who is carrying meat-pies along with him this morning ? I hope it's a friend of mine ! "

Through the trees he went, hoppitty-skip, looking for those pies—and pretty soon he came up to Brer Wolf and Brer Fox.

" Howdy ! " said Brer Rabbit.

" Howdy ! " said Brer Fox and Brer Wolf, stopping.

" Good pies you've got there ! " said Brer Rabbit, sniffing hungrily.

"Would you like a piece of mine?" asked Brer Fox politely, and he set his rod down on the ground and put his pie on a tree-stump.

Well, Brer Rabbit was so mighty keen to eat a bit of that pie that he didn't see the wicked look in Brer Fox's eye, and he went a bit nearer.

"Come along, Brer Rabbit, you help yourself to a slice," said Brer Fox generously. "Have you got a knife? Cut yourself what you want."

Brer Rabbit took out his knife and went up to the pie. "It's mighty kind of you, Brer Fox," he said. "I always did say you were——"

But what he was going to say nobody ever knew, for just at that minute Brer Wolf grabbed at Brer Rabbit's coat and held on for all he was worth!

"Got him!" he said to Brer Fox, with a grin. "Talk about pies, Brer Fox—we'll be having rabbit-pie to-night all right!"

Brer Rabbit was mighty scared. He looked round at Brer Wolf. "Let me go, please, sir," he said. "I've done you no harm. And that's my new coat you're pulling at."

"New coat or old coat, it's what I'm holding you by!"

grinned Brer Wolf. But that's just where old Brer Wolf was wrong—for in a trice Brer Rabbit had wriggled his arms out of his coat and was tearing off through the wood as fast as he could go, leaving his empty coat in Brer Wolf's hands.

"After him, after him!" yelled Brer Fox, who couldn't bear to see his rabbit-pie running away like that. So both Brer Wolf and Brer Fox tore after Brer Rabbit, making the dead leaves fly in the air as they went.

Soon Brer Rabbit came to the stream. It was full and deep. He couldn't swim it. There was no boat. What was he to do? Quick as lightning he picked up a heavy stone and flung it into the water, just as Brer Wolf and Brer Fox came into sight. Then Brer Rabbit slipped into a hollow tree and sat there all a-tremble.

"He's jumped into the stream!" cried Brer Fox. "Look, there's the round ripple he made. He'll drown!"

"Well, we'll wait till he comes floating to the top and we'll get him," said Brer Wolf, sitting down. "My, what a splash he made, didn't he! Well, well—it's the end of him to-day—and good riddance too. I'm just about tired of being tricked by that cheeky rabbit."

"We may as well do a bit of fishing whilst we are waiting for Brer Rabbit to come up," said Brer Fox, fixing his rod. He put down his pie behind him and Brer Wolf did the same. Then they both began to fish.

"Funny that Brer Rabbit doesn't come floating to the top," said Brer Wolf, after a bit. "I guess he must have got caught on some weeds at the bottom."

"Maybe Brer Terrapin will find him," said Brer Fox. "We'll ask him when we see him."

Well, Brer Rabbit was sitting just behind Brer Fox and Brer Wolf in the hollow tree. He grinned when he heard what they said. He quietly put out a paw and took Brer Fox's pie. He sat in the hollow tree and ate it, every crumb. It was delicious. Then he stretched out a paw for Brer Wolf's.

Just then Brer Wolf caught a fish, and he was so excited that he could think of nothing else.

"Just the time for me to slip out, I think!" grinned Brer Rabbit to himself. So out he slipped, carrying Brer Wolf's pie in his hand. He went to a tree-stump a good way off, and sat there, nibbling it.

Pretty soon Brer Bullfrog popped up his head and wished Brer Wolf and Brer Fox good-day.

"Have you heard the news?" asked Brer Wolf. "Brer Rabbit is drowned. He jumped in this stream and we haven't seen him since."

"Dear me," said Brer Bullfrog, astonished. He swam off to tell Brer Terrapin. Presently Brer Terrapin came along with Brer Bullfrog, all upset to hear the news, for he was fond of old Brer Rabbit.

"You say he jumped in this stream and was drowned, Brer Wolf?" he said. "Poor old Brer Rabbit! He was a cheeky creature—but a mighty good friend to me. I'm sorry to hear the news. The world won't be the same now."

"It certainly won't," said Brer Fox. "We shall have a bit of peace, and our things won't be stolen. Brer Wolf, what about a bit of lunch now? I'm hungry. Brer Terrapin, you come along and join us."

Brer Terrapin thought he wouldn't. He kept in the water. He had just seen a most peculiar sight, and he wanted to giggle to himself without being seen.

"Where's my pie?" said Brer Wolf, feeling behind him. It wasn't there—and neither was Brer Fox's! The two animals glared at one another.

"You've taken my pie!" said Brer Wolf.

"I have not," said Brer Fox. "*You*'ve taken mine!"

"Brer Fox, you've sat there and eaten my pie when I was

watching that fish ?" shouted Brer Wolf. "I know you and your tricks !" He gave Brer Fox a blow.

"Stop that !" cried Brer Fox. "First you eat my pie and then you hit me ! You just stop that, Brer Wolf ! I tell you, I haven't eaten your pie !"

"You'll be telling me that poor drowned Brer Rabbit has eaten my pie next, I suppose !" roared Brer Wolf in a rage and he gave Brer Fox such a push that he fell right into the water. But he clutched at Brer Wolf as he went—and old Brer Wolf he fell in with a splash too, right on top of Brer Fox ! Brer Terrapin gave a squeal of laughter and swam off to the other side.

Brer Wolf and Brer Fox came up to the top at the same time. They poked their heads out of the water and choked and spluttered—and the very first thing they saw when they turned their heads towards the nearby bank was old Brer Rabbit sitting up on his tree-stump, nibbling away for all he was worth at Brer Wolf's pie !

"He's not drowned !" yelled Brer Wolf. "He's got my pie ! Quick, Brer Fox, after him, before he eats it all !"

So out they climbed, dripping wet, but by then Brer Rabbit was nowhere to be seen. He didn't wait to say he was sorry—not he ! He was off through the woods, laughing like a green woodpecker, the wicked rascal !

Brer Rabbit and the Tongs

ONCE BRER RABBIT went to get a present for his old woman. She wanted a pair of tongs for the fire, and a nice poker.

" And see you get a *long* poker and a *long* pair of tongs ! " she said. " The fire gets so hot sometimes that I can't get near it to put another log on the fire. A long pair of tongs will save my whiskers getting singed off ! "

So Brer Rabbit went to town and he bought a fine long pair of tongs and a fine long poker. He put the poker under his arm, and hung the tongs round his neck. Then back he went through the woods, whistling like a blackbird.

Old Brer Fox heard the whistling and he knew who it was. He shot along to meet Brer Rabbit, and waited for him behind a tree. He heard him coming along merrily, and he grinned to himself to think what a shock he was going to give Brer Rabbit.

When Brer Rabbit came up to the tree, Brer Fox rushed out like a whirlwind. He pounced on Brer Rabbit and held him fast.

" Now, let go, let go ! " cried old Brer Rabbit in a fright. But Brer Fox didn't mean to let go ! He held Brer Rabbit tightly, and gave him a shake.

The tongs and the poker banged together and made a clanking noise.

" What are those ? " asked Brer Fox in astonishment. He had never seen fire-irons before, and he couldn't imagine what they were.

" Brer Fox, if you let me go, I'll give you these wonderful, marvellous things," said Brer Rabbit at once.

"Why, what do they do?" asked Brer Fox.

"Well, you see this?" said Brer Rabbit, taking the tongs from round his neck, and opening and shutting them. "Now you've only got to say what you want to eat, and you'll see it appear between these tongs, and they'll hold it for you—like that."

Brer Rabbit let the tongs shut with a clang.

"And what's the other thing for?" asked Brer Fox, looking at the long steel poker.

"I'll show you what that's for, when you've seen what the tongs can do," said Brer Rabbit. "Now, Brer Fox, you just let me go, and you can have these marvellous things."

"I'll not let you go till you show me what they do," said Brer Fox firmly. "I've had enough of your tricks, Brer Rabbit. I'm just going to hold on to you till you show me what all these things can do."

"All right, all right," said Brer Rabbit. "I'll show you. Let me open these tongs again—and point them at you—like that. Now, you must shut your eyes and wish for what you want—and maybe when you open them again you'll get a fine surprise!"

"I shall still keep hold of you!" said Brer Fox, and he held Brer Rabbit fast by the sleeve. He shut his eyes and thought of roast duck. If only he could see a roast duck between those tongs when he opened his eyes! "Brer Rabbit said I should get a surprise!" he thought.

He did get a surprise—but it wasn't the surprise he wanted! No—it was a most unpleasant surprise. He suddenly felt something biting his nose hard—squeezing it, pinching it! He let Brer Rabbit go and put his paws up to his poor nose at once, howling and yelling!

He opened his eyes, and saw that the tongs had got hold of his nose. Brer Rabbit was pinching his nose with them as hard as he could. The tongs were so long that once Brer Fox let go Brer Rabbit's sleeve, Brer Rabbit could stand far enough away not to be caught again.

Brer Fox tried to get the tongs off his nose. He tried to grab Brer Rabbit. He howled with rage. He danced about in pain. But Brer Rabbit wouldn't let go!

"Loose me! Loose me!" cried Brer Fox, trying to push the tongs off his nose. "Let me go, let me go!"

"You wanted to know what the tongs were for," said Brer Rabbit, "and now I'm showing you! And you wanted to know what the poker was for, and I'll show you that too!"

And with that Brer Rabbit began to poke poor Brer Fox in the ribs till he howled with rage. Poke, poke, poke!

"Ow, ow, ow!"

Poke, poke, poke!

"Ow, ow, ow!"

"Now get along, please," said Brer Rabbit, still holding Brer Fox with the tongs, and poking him with the poker. "Get along! I've got to get home to dinner, and I'm not staying here all day!"

So poor Brer Fox had to walk backwards, with Brer Rabbit grabbing his long nose with the tongs, and poking him with the poker. When Brer Rabbit got up his front path, he yelled to his wife to open the door.

As soon as it was open, he opened the tongs, let go Brer Fox's nose, slipped inside the door, and bolted it! He looked out of the window.

"So glad you know how to use tongs and poker now!" he called. "Come and call on me again if you ever want another lesson."

Brer Fox didn't answer. He ran off, with his nose in his paws, and asked Brer Bear to bandage it for him. Brer Bear roared with laughter to see him with a bandage round his nose.

"You can't talk and you can't eat!" he said. "You'd better keep out of old Brer Rabbit's way for the next few days, Brer Fox, or he'll kill himself with laughing at you!"

So Brer Fox vanished for a week and nursed his nose. Poor old Brer Fox, he just *can't* get the better of Brer Rabbit!

Brer Fox Sells His Family

NOW, IN the time when things were very bad for all the creatures and they could get nothing to eat, Brer Fox happened to meet old Brer Rabbit.

"Heyo, Brer Rabbit!" said Brer Fox. "Where's our bread coming from next?"

"Looks like it might be coming from nowhere," said Brer Rabbit. Then the two sat down and began to talk about how they could get some food.

"Well, Brer Fox," said Brer Rabbit at last, "we'd better sell our families and buy some corn with the money, and then we'll have something to eat."

"Well, that's fair and square," said Brer Fox. "My old woman and her cubs are a lot of bother. I'd be glad to get rid of them. Yes, Brer Rabbit, we'll take them into town in the wagon and sell them all, both yours and mine."

So they parted and each went back to his family. Brer Fox went home, caught his old woman and the cubs, and tied them all up fast with red twine.

Well, Brer Rabbit went home too—and he grinned and told his family the trick he meant to play on Brer Fox. And they let him catch them and tie them all up fast, and take them along to the road the next morning, where Brer Rabbit had promised to meet Brer Fox.

There was Brer Fox with the wagon. He sat up on the driving seat, and his family was all underneath the seat, tied up tightly. Brer Rabbit put his own family in the back of the wagon.

"I'd better sit here at the back with my family, Brer Fox!"

called old Brer Rabbit, " else they'll start to squall. They'll be all right in a little while, once we get going ! "

So Brer Fox cracked his whip, clucked to the horses and set off towards town. And every little while Brer Fox shouted to Brer Rabbit : " You awake, Brer Rabbit ? No nodding back there, now ! "

Then Brer Rabbit would shout back, " You look after the rocks and ruts in the road, Brer Fox, and I'll look after the nodding ! "

But all the time, bless gracious ! Brer Rabbit was sitting quietly untying his old woman and seven children ! When he had them all untied Brer Rabbit went and sat by Brer Fox on the driving seat, and they talked and laughed about all sorts of things and planned what they were going to do with the corn they got in exchange for their families.

" I shall bake myself a hoe-cake ! " said Brer Fox.

" And I shall make a ginger cake ! " said Brer Rabbit.

Just about then one of Brer Rabbit's children lifted himself up and hopped out of the wagon. He ran away into the woods, lippitty-clippitty !

Miss Fox saw him and she sang out :

" One from seven
Don't leave eleven."

Brer Fox pushed his old woman with his foot to make her keep quiet. By and by another little rabbit popped up and hopped out of the wagon—and away into the woods he went, lippitty-clippitty!

Miss Fox saw him and sang out:

> *"One from six*
> *Leaves me less kicks!"*

Brer Fox took no notice. He went on talking to Brer Rabbit, and Brer Rabbit went on answering him, and before very long another of Brer Rabbit's children hopped out and ran off.

> *"One from five*
> *Leaves four alive!"*

sang out Miss Fox, and Brer Fox pushed her again to make her stop talking. Then another rabbit went and Miss Fox sang out:

> *"One from four*
> *Leaves three and no more!"*

And when the next rabbit went she said:

> *"One from three*
> *Leaves two to go free."*

And when the last little rabbit went she sang out:

> *"One from one*
> *And they're all gone!"*

And then Brer Rabbit's old woman hopped out and went too! So when Brer Fox happened to look round he was mighty astonished to see no rabbits there at all!

He pulled at the reins and shouted, "Wo! Wo! In the name of goodness, Brer Rabbit, where is all your family?"

Brer Rabbit looked round, and then he put his paws up to

his face and pretended he was crying. He just fairly boo-hooed, and said: " There now, Brer Fox! I knew if I put my poor little children in there with your family they'd be eaten up! I just knew it!"

Well, old Miss Fox she vowed and declared she hadn't touched Brer Rabbit's family. But Brer Fox didn't believe her. He had been wanting a bite of those little rabbits so badly that he got mighty mad with his old woman and the children and said: " Well, say what you like, I'm a going to get rid of you this very day!"

And sure enough he took his whole family to town, sold them and bought two big bags of corn with the money.

" You've got to give me one of those bags of corn," said Brer Rabbit. " You've sold my family as well as your own, don't forget, because yours has eaten mine! So give me a bag of corn, Brer Fox, or I'll start a-weeping till I get cold in my feet with the puddles I'll make!"

So Brer Fox gave him a bag of corn and Brer Rabbit, he set off with it as fast as he could, and he didn't stop till he got home. And there was his old woman waiting for him with the pot boiling and a big fire going—and all his little rabbits clapping their paws in delight to see the big bag of corn.

Oh, Brer Rabbit—you're too smart for anything! One of these days you'll get caught, for sure!

Brer Bear's Turnips

NOW ONCE Brer Bear met Brer Rabbit going home with a sack over his shoulder. Brer Bear didn't like the look of it at all, because Brer Rabbit was walking out of Brer Bear's field, and old Brer Bear felt sure that Brer Rabbit was up to no good.

"What have you got in that sack, Brer Rabbit?" asked Brer Bear.

"Turnips, Brer Bear, turnips," answered Brer Rabbit saucily. "Do you know what turnips are? If you don't, I'll be pleased to show you."

"Brer Rabbit, I know what turnips are, and what's more, I know my own turnips when I see them," said Brer Bear. "I believe you've been digging up my turnips."

"Brer Bear, they are my own turnips, dug up out of my field, and I'm only walking through *your* field because it's a short cut to my home," said Brer Rabbit.

"What do you want with a sack of turnips?" asked Brer Bear. "Didn't I see plenty in your shed the other day? You can't have used them all up."

"Brer Bear, I haven't used them all up, and since you are so mighty curious about these turnips I will tell you what I am going to do with them," said Brer Rabbit. "My old aunt has a birthday to-morrow, and I am going to pack these turnips into a nice box, tie it up with pretty paper and ribbon, and take them to her for her birthday! Now, are you satisfied?"

Brer Bear grunted and went off. He wasn't at all sure that they were not his turnips—and when he came to a newly-dug bit of his field, where turnips had been taken, he was furious.

He looked back after Brer Rabbit, and made up his mind that he would get those turnips back somehow!

"I'll steal along there to-night and take the parcel when Brer Rabbit has done it up nicely," thought old Brer Bear. "Yes, that's what I'll do. Hallo, there's Brer Terrapin. I'll tell him all about that scamp of a Brer Rabbit."

So he told Brer Terrapin all about how Brer Rabbit had taken his turnips, and how he was going to wait till Brer Rabbit had done them up into a neat parcel and then he was going to take the parcel and all!

"That'll teach him to take my turnips, won't it!" said Brer Bear, with a grunt. Brer Terrapin laughed and moved off. He was Brer Rabbit's friend, and he meant to warn him of what Brer Bear had said.

Well, when Brer Rabbit heard what old Brer Terrapin had to tell him, he laughed and laughed.

"I didn't take his turnips," he said. "They were my own. Old Miss Bear came along and dug up some of Brer Bear's turnips to make soup for him. Ho, ho! so Brer Bear is going to come along this evening and take my parcel, is he? Well, he can come, yes, he can come all right!

Now, as soon as it grew dark that night, Brer Rabbit did a very funny thing. He slipped out of his house and went along to Brer Bear's as quietly as a shadow. And when he got to the front door, he didn't knock! No, he did something else instead!

He quietly unscrewed Brer Bear's knocker from the front door and put it into his pocket. Then he picked up the door-mat and put it over one shoulder, and he picked up the shoe-scraper and put that under his arm. Then he walked off home with the whole lot!

And when he got there he set the things on his table, got out his pretty paper and a box, and packed up the knocker, the door-mat and the shoe-scraper into the box. He wrapped them up in the pretty paper and tied them up with red string.

Then he set the box on the kitchen table, and opened the window. He went out of the room and left the door a little bit open so that he could see through the crack.

Pretty soon, along came old Brer Bear. He peeped in at the open window and saw the parcel neatly set out on the table. He gave a big grin and clambered over the sill. This was much easier than he had expected!

He picked up the parcel and put it on his shoulder.

My, it was heavy! What big turnips they must be! Then out of the window went old Brer Bear, and off home, whilst Brer Rabbit nearly died of laughing, peeping through the crack of the door!

Now when Brer Bear reached home, his old woman met him at the door in a dreadful state.

"Brer Bear, oh, Brer Bear, someone's been along and stolen my knocker and my door-mat and my shoe-scraper! Oh, I'm so unhappy! I did love that bright knocker so much, and the door-mat was new, and the shoe-scraper cost such a lot of money! Oh my, oh my, what am I to do? You go and catch the thief at once!"

"Wait, wait," said Brer Bear, putting down his parcel with a bump. "How can I catch the thief if I don't know who he is? Don't be such a silly old woman. Look—I've brought you some turnips—the ones that Brer Rabbit dug out of my field to-day."

"*I* dug those turnips, not Brer Rabbit," said Miss Bear. "Well, well, we've a lot of turnips to eat now, that's certain. I guess Brer Rabbit won't thank you when he finds out that you've walked off with his turnips!"

Miss Bear took a knife and cut the string of the parcel. She took off the paper. She opened the box—and out tumbled her knocker, her door-mat, and her shoe-scraper. She gave a scream.

"Brer Bear! You've played a trick on me, you have! These aren't turnips! They are the things from my front door! You're playing a trick on me, you bad, wicked bear!"

And with that old Miss Bear caught hold of Brer Bear and smacked him so hard on one ear that he bellowed in pain. He ran out of his front door—and bumped into Brer Rabbit, who was passing by to take his parcel of turnips to his old aunt.

"Now, now!" said Brer Rabbit, "what's the sense of rushing about and knocking people over! You nearly knocked this birthday parcel out of my hands! I wouldn't like my old aunt's turnips to be spoilt!"

Brer Bear stopped still and glared at Brer Rabbit and the box wrapped up in pretty paper. It was just exactly like the parcel he had taken from Brer Rabbit's kitchen table!

"You—you—you—rogue!" spluttered poor Brer Bear. "You wicked scamp, Brer Rabbit!"

"Brer Bear, I'd just like to know why you are calling me names?" said Brer Rabbit in a furious voice.

And then Brer Bear found that he couldn't tell him—because if he did, he would have to say that he had taken a parcel from Brer Rabbit's kitchen table! So he just had to hold his tongue and say nothing at all, though he nearly burst with rage!

Brer Rabbit went off, head in air and parcel on shoulder. He whistled merrily, and when he wasn't whistling, he grinned. As for Brer Bear, he went grunting and growling into his house, and then had to spend half an hour trying to put his knocker back on his front door again!

Brer Wolf's Supper

NOW ONCE, when Brer Fox and Brer Wolf were going home after a day's fishing, they came across Old Brer Rabbit fast asleep under a frond of bracken. Brer Rabbit had been working in his garden all day and he was tired out.

"Ho! Look at that!" said Brer Wolf, who saw Brer Rabbit first. "Do you suppose he really *is* asleep? Or do you think he's pretending and will jump up as soon as we get near?"

"Well, we'll see!" said Brer Fox. "You go that side, Brer Wolf, and I'll go the other. Then we'll pounce together and see if we can't get the rascal. It's time he was caught, no doubt about that!"

So Brer Wolf crept on one side of Brer Rabbit and Brer Fox crept to the other. They both pounced together—but Brer Wolf got him, and held him fast in his big paws!

Brer Rabbit woke up with a jump and blinked in fright at Brer Wolf.

"Got you at last!" said Brer Wolf, pleased.

"Oh, please, sir, let me go! Oh, please, sir, let me go!" begged Brer Rabbit, who was really very frightened.

"What shall we do with him?" asked Brer Wolf. "My old woman will cook these fishes for us for dinner—but maybe we could have Brer Rabbit for supper."

"A very good idea," said Brer Fox. "But how can we carry him home when we've got all these fish to take and our rods too?"

"We won't take him with us," said Brer Wolf, looking around. "We'll put him somewhere till tonight."

"What about in that little cave over there?" said Brer Fox, pointing.

"Yes, you put me in there," said Brer Rabbit, at once. "I'll be safe there, especially if you put a big stone at the opening so that I can't get away."

"We don't want to hear any advice from *you*, Brer Rabbit," said Brer Wolf firmly. "And as for that cave, I'd not be such a silly as to put any rabbit there. Why, Brer Fox, he'd burrow out of there in two or three minutes."

"Yes, that's true," said Brer Fox, looking rather foolish. "Well, where do *you* suggest, Brer Wolf?"

"There's a good hole in that tree over there," said Brer Wolf, still holding poor Brer Rabbit by his ears. "We could stuff him in there, and put a big pile of stones over the opening so that he couldn't possibly get out. That's what we'll do!"

"Oh, please, sir, let me go!" squeaked Brer Rabbit.

Brer Wolf took no notice at all. He carried Brer Rabbit to the tree and stuffed him into a small hole at the bottom. Then he and Brer Fox piled stones over the entrance so that Brer Rabbit couldn't possibly get out.

"There!" he said, pleased. "We've hidden our supper well! We'll fetch it to-night, Brer Fox."

They went off—but they did not know that Brer Coon had come up and had been watching them pile the stones over the hole. Brer Coon hadn't seen Brer Rabbit—he had only heard what Brer Wolf had said before he went.

"Ho!" said Brer Coon, his sharp eyes looking at the heap of stones. "They've hidden their supper there, have they? Well, weil! What's a hungry coon to do when he hears there's a nice supper waiting in the hollow of a tree?"

Brer Coon waited until Brer Fox and Brer Wolf had gone, and then he ran to the tree and began sniffing around the stones.

He could smell no supper—but strangely enough he could smell rabbit! And live rabbit, too! Very queer.

At last he heard a tiny noise, and then Brer Coon was certain that Brer Rabbit was in there. But what was he doing there? Was he eating Brer Wolf's supper? Brer Rabbit was clever enough for anything.

Brer Coon called softly, "Brer Rabbit! Brer Rabbit! Are you in there?"

"Yes, that I am," answered Brer Rabbit at once.

"Brer Wolf said his supper was in there, Brer Rabbit," said Brer Coon. "Are you eating it, Brer Rabbit? Is there a bit for me? I'm very hungry this morning."

"Why, if that isn't dear old Brer Coon!" said Brer Rabbit, in a hearty voice. "Of course you can share in the food, Brer Coon. Come right along in!"

"But how?" asked Brer Coon. "I don't see any way in. How did *you* get in, Brer Rabbit?"

"Ah, that's giving away a secret," said Brer Rabbit. "If you want to come in, you'll have to pull away a few of those stones, Brer Coon. Then you can creep in quite easily."

Brer Coon puffed and panted as he pulled at the big stones, but one by one he managed to roll them away, and at last he had uncovered the hole enough to squeeze into it.

But before he could so much as put his head inside, Brer

Rabbit rushed out like a gale of wind, and knocked poor Brer Coon right over. He went spinning over the bracken, and all the breath was knocked out of his body.

"Sorry, Brer Coon!" shouted Brer Rabbit. "I've just remembered that I've got to get home quickly. You go in and eat all you can find!"

Brer Coon crept in at the hole—but sniff as he might, not a crumb of supper could he find. He was very angry indeed with Brer Rabbit.

"The mean creature!" he said, as he padded home. "He's eaten the lot! I've a good mind to tell Brer Wolf!"

So when he did come across Brer Wolf running along to the tree to get Brer Rabbit for his supper, Brer Coon told him.

"Brer Rabbit's eaten all the supper you left in that tree," said Brer Coon. Brer Wolf stopped and stared at Brer Coon.

"How do you know?" asked Brer Wolf, looking dangerous.

"Well, you see," began Brer Coon, edging away a little, "when I pulled the stones away from the hole . . ."

"When you *what*?" roared Brer Wolf, and he sprang in rage at Brer Coon. But old Brer Coon was a wily one, and he slipped to one side and disappeared like a shadow.

As for old Brer Rabbit, he stayed at home for two days. He had had a shock—but all the same he grinned and grinned when he thought of poor Brer Coon hunting in the tree for Brer Wolf's supper

Brer Rabbit's Meat

Now it got about that Brer Rabbit had gone off with Brer Fox's sacks of food, and all the other creatures kept a sharp eye on him, hoping to get some of the food out of him. But, bless gracious, Brer Rabbit was too smart for them, and not a coffee bean did any one get—no, not so much as the smell of it!

One morning one of Brer Rabbit's children came running in to tell him that he had found a big piece of meat lying in the woods. Brer Rabbit pricked up his big ears, tied his scarf round his neck and set off to find it. Sure enough there was a fine piece of meat there, and Brer Rabbit did a dance of joy.

But just as he was about to carve it up to take home, old Brer Wolf happened along.

"Heyo, Brer Rabbit!" he said, as he smelt the meat. "So this is where you keep your stores! My, that's a fine piece of meat! If you ask me to have a bite, I won't say no—and if you don't ask me, well, I'll have some all the same!"

And with that he set to work, carving and cutting at the meat, glad to pay Brer Rabbit out for all the tricks he had played on him.

"We'll share this meat between us, Brer Rabbit," he said. "But as I'm the biggest, it's fair I should have more than you, isn't it?"

Well, by the way Brer Wolf set to work at that meat, it looked as if he would eat it all! Brer Rabbit put on a don't-care look, but he was so upset that he really felt bad! He walked all round the meat, he did, and sniffed the air—and soon he said:

"Brer Wolf! Brer Wolf! Does this meat smell really good to you?"

Brer Wolf went on cutting and carving, and didn't say a word. Then Brer Rabbit walked all round the meat once more. He poked it with his paw. He kicked it.

"Brer Wolf! Oh, Brer Wolf!" he said, "this meat feels mighty flabby to me. How does it feel to you?"

Brer Wolf heard every word that was said, but he kept on cutting and carving.

"Well," said Brer Rabbit, "you can talk or not talk, Brer Wolf, just as you please—but if I'm not mistaken in the smell, you'll be very sorry for yourself before you've finished this beef! You just wait and see, Brer Wolf!"

With that Brer Rabbit set off to his home and pretty soon came back with a dish of salt and a piece of burning wood.

Brer Wolf looked up in surprise. "What are you going to do with all that, Brer Rabbit?"

Brer Rabbit laughed as if he knew a lot more than he would tell. "Bless gracious, Brer Wolf! I'm not going to take even a pound of this meat home till I find out what's wrong with it. No, I'm not—so there now!"

Then Brer Rabbit built a fire of twigs and branches, lighted it with his piece of burning wood, and cut himself a slice of the meat. He held it over the fire till it was well broiled, and then he ate a little of it.

First he'd taste and then he'd nibble; then he'd nibble and then he'd taste. He kept on till he had eaten a good piece of the meat. Then he went and sat a little way off as if he were waiting for something.

Brer Wolf went on carving and cutting, but he kept one eye on Brer Rabbit. Brer Rabbit sat up straight as a judge. Brer Wolf watched him carefully. Soon Brer Rabbit flung both of his hands up to his head and gave a deep groan. Brer Wolf cut and carved, and watched Brer Rabbit. Then Brer

Rabbit began to sway backwards and forwards, and groaned and moaned all the time. Then he swayed from side to side.

"Oh my, oh my, oh my!" he groaned. "Oh my!"

Well, Brer Wolf began to feel a bit scared at all this. "What's the matter?" he said.

Then Brer Rabbit rolled over and over on the ground and yelled: "Oh my, oh my! I'm poisoned, I'm poisoned! Oh my! I'm poisoned! Run and fetch the doctor, somebody! Run and fetch the doctor! Help! Help! The meat's got poison on it! Oh, help! help!"

Well, Brer Wolf was so scared that he set off at once to fetch the doctor, and he was no sooner out of sight than up jumped Brer Rabbit, grinning from whisker to whisker, and began to cut up that meat as fast as ever he could!

He ran to and from his smoke-house with big pieces, and it wasn't very long before Brer Rabbit had got every bit safely put away, and the smoke-house door shut and bolted!

Well, Brer Wolf found the doctor and told him all about poor Brer Rabbit, and how he had been poisoned—and Brer Wolf was pretty scared himself too, thinking he might be poisoned as well! Brer Wolf hurried back with the doctor, and when he got there Brer Rabbit and the meat had gone. And, bless goodness, if it hadn't been for Brer Rabbit's fire which was still burning, Brer Wolf would have found it very difficult to find where the meat had been at all!

And whenever Brer Wolf passed Brer Rabbit's house that week he could smell fried meat and onions a-cooking. But old Brer Wolf didn't get more than the smell of it, for Brer Rabbit was mighty careful to keep his door locked for a month of Sundays afterwards!

Brer Rabbit has an Idea

It seemed as if Brer Rabbit always came out on top of everybody, even Mr. Man, he was so cunning and tricky—but there was one time when he got laughed at by all the other creatures.

There was some sort of squabble among the creatures, and they held a meeting to see if they could make it up. When the time came for the meeting they were all there, and they sat down and began to talk. All of them had something to say, and they talked as if they were paid for talking! They each had a plan, and they jabbered at the top of their voices.

Now, Mr. Dog was there, and he took a seat just by Brer Rabbit. When Mr. Dog opened his mouth to say something Brer Rabbit saw his teeth, so long and strong, and they shone so white that Brer Rabbit felt mighty scared.

Mr. Dog spoke, and Brer Rabbit jumped as if he was afraid Mr. Dog was going to snap at him. He jumped and he dodged down. Mr. Dog laughed, and that made Brer Rabbit jump again, because he saw all Mr. Dog's teeth when he laughed. Well, it went on like this, and every time Mr. Dog spoke or laughed Brer Rabbit jumped and dodged till the creatures clapped their hands together and laughed fit to kill themselves.

Mr. Dog thought they were laughing at *him*, and this made him mad. He growled and he snapped, and this gave poor

Brer Rabbit such a terrible scare that he dropped down off his chair and hid underneath it.

Of course this made all the creatures laugh more than ever, and the more they laughed the madder Mr. Dog got, till by and by he got so mad that he howled, and poor Brer Rabbit sat under his chair shaking and trembling like a leaf in the wind !

After a while Brer Rabbit slipped across to the other side of the room, and then he got up and made a speech.

" I say we ought to make it a law that all creatures with big teeth should catch their food with their claws and not their jaws," said Brer Rabbit.

Well, everyone agreed to this except Mr. Dog, Brer Wolf and Brer Fox. In those days if all the creatures didn't agree they put it off till the next meeting, and talked it over some more, and that's what they did with Brer Rabbit's idea. They put it off till the next meeting.

Brer Rabbit had a sort of feeling that the creatures were not going to agree to his idea. So when he next met Brer Wolf he said to him that he thought the best thing to do to get everyone to agree would be to have Mr. Dog's mouth sewn up, because his teeth looked so fierce.

" That's a mighty fine idea of yours," said Brer Wolf, who

was no friend of Mr. Dog's. " We'll all agree to that at the next meeting."

Sure enough, when the day came, Brer Rabbit got up and said that the best thing to do with Mr. Dog to stop him catching his food with his teeth would be to sew up his mouth. Then his teeth wouldn't look so fierce. Everyone agreed to this and clapped the idea loudly.

Then Mr. Lion spoke up from his big armchair. " And who's going to do the sewing ? " he said.

Everyone looked at somebody else. Then Brer Wolf grinned and spoke. " The man that wants the sewing done is the man who ought to do it ! " he said. " Then he'll know it's done right ! "

Brer Rabbit got a shock when he heard this. If there was one thing he didn't want to do, it was to get near Mr. Dog's teeth. So he sat and thought hard, and then he said :

" I haven't got a needle."

Brer Bear felt about in the flap of his coat-collar and found a needle.

" Here, Brer Rabbit. Here's a great big one ! "

Brer Rabbit took the needle and thought mighty hard again.

" I haven't got any thread," he said.

Brer Bear pulled a thread from the bottom of his woolly waistcoat and held it out to Brer Rabbit.

" Here, Brer Rabbit. Here's a great long one ! "

Now anyone else but Brer Rabbit wouldn't have been able to think of any way of getting out of such a fix. But old Brer Rabbit, he just rubbed his nose, got up from his chair, threaded the needle with the wool and said :

" Well, I'm ready now, and I see Mr. Dog a-sitting over there waiting. Brer Bear, just hold him still for me, will you, whilst I sew up his mouth."

Well, Brer Bear, he stared at Brer Rabbit as if he couldn't believe his ears. Hold Mr. Dog ? Not he !

"I'm off to see how my old woman is," he said. "She was poorly this morning!" And off he lumbered.

"Bless gracious!" said Brer Rabbit, looking after him. "He's scared, that's what he is! Brer Wolf, you come along and hold Mr. Dog for me. I won't be long sewing up his mouth."

Brer Wolf looked scared. "I would do it for you, Brer Rabbit," said he, "but I've got a thorn in one of my paws this morning."

"What about you, Brer Fox?" said Brer Rabbit.

"Oh, Brer Rabbit, don't ask me such a thing!" said Brer Fox. "I've got work to do to-day that won't wait another minute!" And off he went to join Brer Bear and Brer Wolf in the woods.

Brer Rabbit looked all round and saw that everyone was looking scared. "Huh!" he said, throwing down the needle and thread, "what's the good of me being brave enough to sew up Mr. Dog's mouth if nobody's got pluck enough to help me!"

At that time Mr. Dog gave a growl—and it wasn't more than half a minute before Brer Rabbit was out of the house and right at the other side of the woods as fast as his legs could carry him! Oho! Brer Rabbit wasn't so brave as he made out, not by a long way.

Brer Rabbit's Honey

Now one day, when Brer Rabbit went to get a pot of honey out of his shed, he saw that half of it was gone.

" Look at that, now ! " said Brer Rabbit, very angry. " Who's been stealing my honey pots ? Yes—one, two, three, four, five, six of them. All gone. Only three left ! "

Brer Rabbit stood still a minute, and then he looked in the mud outside the door. In the mud he saw the print of Brer Bear's big feet, claws and all.

" Oho, Brer Bear, so *you've* been along here after my honey, have you ! " said Brer Rabbit, to himself. " Well, you think yourself mighty clever, don't you, taking honey from old Brer Rabbit. But I'll get it back, or I'll eat my whiskers ! "

So Brer Rabbit hid himself outside Brer Bear's house, waiting for old Brer Bear to go walking out, so that he might slip inside and find his pots of honey. But whenever Brer Bear stepped out, he left old Miss Bear behind in the house—and she was every bit as big and fierce as Brer Bear himself.

" This won't do," said Brer Rabbit to himself. " If I don't get that honey soon, it'll be gone—and I'll have to eat my own whiskers."

He sat and thought. He scratched his head, and he pulled at his whiskers. Then he slapped his knee, and gave a grin. It didn't take Brer Rabbit long to think of a trick—he was just full of them, any time of night or day !

Old Brer Rabbit ambled off till he came to the riverside. He whistled, and up came Uncle Mud-Turtle, a-bubbling under the water.

" Good morning to you," said Brer Rabbit. " I'd take it

mighty kind of you if you'd do something for me, Uncle Mud-Turtle."

"I'll bubble-bubble-bubble do it," answered Uncle Mud-Turtle.

"Well, listen, now," said Brer Rabbit. "There's a mighty cosy hole just here, and I want you to sit in it, Uncle Mud-Turtle, and if anything comes down this hole, well, you just hold on to it for all you're worth. See? You just do that, and I'll give you a taste of the finest honey you ever sipped!"

"Bubble-bubble," answered Uncle Mud-Turtle. He got himself into the cosy hole by the bank and settled down comfortably to wait. Brer Rabbit sat by the hole too, and he watched till he saw Brer Bear coming out of his house. Then Brer Rabbit began to whistle very gently, as if he was humming a tune all to himself.

Brer Bear heard him and came through the bushes. He saw Brer Rabbit with his paw just coming out of the hole, and he spoke to him.

"What are you doing there, Brer Rabbit?"

"Oh, is it you, Brer Bear?" said Brer Rabbit, standing up quickly and brushing himself down. "I wasn't doing anything much."

"You just tell me what you were doing now, Brer Rabbit," said Brer Bear, moving closer.

"Well, don't you tell anyone if I tell you, Brer Bear," begged Brer Rabbit.

"You go on and tell me," said Brer Bear.

"Well, Brer Bear, it's like this," said cunning old Brer Rabbit. "Some one has been stealing my honey. It might be Brer Fox and it might be Brer Wolf. So I'm looking for a place to hide it safely. Would you think this hole a good place, Brer Bear?"

"Oh, a mighty good place," said Brer Bear at once. "Have you put any there yet, Brer Rabbit?"

"Oh, I shan't tell you *that*," said Brer Rabbit. "You won't go and tell anyone, will you, Brer Bear?"

"Not I," said Brer Bear, making up his mind to look in that hole as soon as Brer Rabbit had gone.

"Well, good-bye, Brer Bear. So nice to have seen you. *Such* a surprise!" said Brer Rabbit, and he skipped nimbly away into the bushes. He hid behind a tree and watched.

Brer Bear waited for a minute or two and then he went to the hole. He sniffed around it, and then put his big paw down to feel about for pots of honey.

And Uncle Mud-Turtle got hold of it and bit it hard! My, how he bit it! And he held on for all he was worth, biting away like a trap!

Brer Bear began to howl. He tried to get his paw out, but Uncle Mud-Turtle bit harder. Brer Bear lifted his head and

yowled like fifty dogs and cats at once. Brer Rabbit slipped to Brer Bear's house and knocked on the door. Miss Bear opened it.

"Miss Bear, quick! Brer Bear's shouting for you!" cried Brer Rabbit.

"But he said I wasn't to leave the house," said Miss Bear.

"Well, you listen to him," said Brer Rabbit. So Miss Bear listened, and when she heard the shouts and yells, the screeches and the howls, she set off down the path to the river just as fast as she could go, crying, "I'm a-coming, I'm a-coming!"

And then Brer Rabbit popped in at Brer Bear's door, saw his honey-pots on the shelf, put them into a basket, and ran out with them. On his way by the river he spied Brer Bear and Miss Bear coming towards him. Brer Bear was nursing his right paw, and howling and crying.

"Why, Brer Bear, what's wrong?" cried Brer Rabbit, standing at a safe distance.

"What's wrong? Plenty wrong!" shouted back Brer Bear. "There's a wild animal down that hole, that's what's wrong. He's eaten your honey, sure enough!"

"Well, I've plenty here!" yelled back Brer Rabbit, and he held up his basket of pots.

Brer Bear knew the basket—and he knew the pots! He gave a yell and rushed towards Brer Rabbit. "You give me back that honey!" he shouted.

"I'll hide it down that hole!" cried Brer Rabbit, dodging away. "You go look for it there, Brer Bear!"

And the funny thing was that old Brer Rabbit *did* hide his honey down that hole—for he guessed that Brer Bear would never dare to put his paw down there again, so it would be as safe there as anywhere!

As for Uncle Mud-Turtle he got his spoonful of honey, but he laughed so much when he took it that he choked and Brer Rabbit had to bang him on the back, and nearly broke his shell! Well, well—you never know what old Brer Rabbit will be up to next!

Brer Rabbit's Bone

ONCE Brer Rabbit went digging carrots in Brer Wolf's garden-patch. This was a mighty dangerous thing to do, for although Brer Wolf was easy to see if he came along, he wasn't easy to hear.

Brer Rabbit took a funny thing along with him each time he went digging for carrots. He took a great big bone and before he dug for any carrots, he buried the bone just nearby.

Well, he went every morning early, before Brer Wolf was up—and it wasn't long before old Brer Wolf found out that his carrots were going.

"That's Brer Rabbit," he growled. "Just because I took a few of his turnips, he's going to dig up the whole of my carrot-field! Well—he's made a mistake this time! I'll catch him, or my name isn't Brer Wolf!"

So he laid a little trap for Brer Rabbit. He put his barrow in the field and piled it with straw—and before dawn one morning Brer Wolf squeezed himself into his big barrow and pulled the straw over him.

There he waited for old Brer Rabbit to come along—and soon along he came, hoppity-skipping, humming a little tune.

He saw the barrow not far off, but he didn't think Brer Wolf was in it. "Careless of somebody to leave their barrow out all night," said Brer Rabbit. He took a quick look round, saw that the curtains were drawn closely over Brer Wolf's windows, and then set to work.

As usual he buried the enormous bone first. Then he began to dig up the carrots and put them into his basket, humming all the time, for he felt very gay and bright that morning.

He didn't see the straw move in the big barrow. He didn't see old Brer Wolf's sharp eyes peering at him. He didn't hear him creep from the barrow and come silently over the field. No—Brer Rabbit didn't see or hear a thing, for his back was to the barrow, and he felt quite sure that Brer Wolf was asleep and snoring.

Wooof! Brer Wolf gave a howl and pounced on Brer Rabbit so suddenly that Brer Rabbit hadn't even time to squeal.

"Got you!" said Brer Wolf in delight. "You wicked fellow, stealing my carrots like this!"

"Well, who took my turnips?" squealed Brer Rabbit, wriggling. "It serves you right."

"And now I'm going to serve *you* right!" said Brer Wolf. "I shouldn't have thought you would have risked being caught by me for the sake of a few carrots, Brer Rabbit."

"You're right," said Brer Rabbit. "It wasn't for the sake of a few carrots. I'm looking for the bone of the Great Winkle-Pip. Whoever eats it becomes three times as strong as they were before—and, as you know, Brer Wolf, I'm only a weak creature, and I thought it would be grand to get as strong as you and Brer Bear."

"Never heard of the Great Winkle-Pip in my life," said Brer Wolf in a disbelieving sort of voice. "You're just making that up to make me think you weren't really after my carrots."

"Oh, Brer Wolf, of course I was after your carrots," said Brer Rabbit. "But I was *really* looking for the great big bone—and just taking the carrots that I dug up in looking for the bone! The funny thing is, I really believe I was somewhere near the bone this morning. I could smell it!"

"I don't believe you," said Brer Wolf, and this was not surprising considering that Brer Rabbit had told many a marvellous story before, to deceive his enemies.

"Ah—wait a minute—I believe I could smell it on the wind just then!" said Brer Rabbit, pretending to get all excited. "Can't you smell it, Brer Wolf?"

"No, I can't—and what's more, *you* can't either!" said Brer Wolf. Then he, too, began to sniff—and sure enough, he did get a whiff of the enormous bone that Brer Rabbit had buried nearby.

"It's funny," said Brer Wolf, sniffing hard, "but I think I *can* smell something now! Well—you just dig up the earth around us a bit, Brer Rabbit, and see if you can find this astonishing bone. Then I'll have a fine bone for my breakfast, and a skinny rabbit for my dinner!"

Brer Rabbit began to dig around a bit, but Brer Wolf kept a paw on his coat-collar all the time. He wasn't going to let Brer Rabbit escape. Not he! Brer Wolf had been tricked too often to let him go this time.

Well, pretty soon Brer Rabbit came to the big bone he had buried. He began to scrape the earth away from it. He put his hand into his pocket and took out a small tube of glue. Brer Wolf was looking in excitement at the end of the big bone, which was now sticking out of the ground. He didn't notice Brer Rabbit's sly movements!

Brer Rabbit went on digging with his right hand, but with his left he squeezed strong glue over the middle of the bone till the tube was empty. Ah—Brer Rabbit always had some trick or other!

At last the great big bone was up. Brer Rabbit grinned at Brer Wolf. "There you are!" he said. "The bone of the Great Winkle-Pip! Let me have a chew at it, Brer Wolf."

"Certainly not," said Brer Wolf. "Do I want you to be three times as strong? No! You'd wriggle away as easy as can be, then! Give that bone to me, Brer Rabbit. I'll soon chew it up—and then I'll be so mighty strong that I'll be able to throw Brer Bear right over the roof of his house if he so much as winks at me!"

Brer Rabbit heaved a great sigh and handed the bone to Brer Wolf. Brer Wolf pushed it into his strong mouth and began to chew—but the glue stuck to his teeth, and in a moment or two he found that he couldn't undo his top and bottom teeth from the bone. They were stuck tight!

"Ooogle-oogle-oogle-oogle!" mumbled Brer Wolf in a fright. He couldn't talk properly, of course. He glared at Brer Rabbit. He tried his best to bite that bone to bits—but he couldn't move his jaws at all!

He put up his paws to take the bone from his mouth—and that was just what old Brer Rabbit was waiting for! In a trice he skipped away, picked up his basket of carrots, and waved good-bye to Brer Wolf.

"You'll soon be three times as strong, Brer Wolf, if you go on chewing that bone!" he cried. "Bite it, bite it!"

"Ooogle-oogle," said poor Brer Wolf, trying his hardest to pull the sticky bone from his mouth. How he pulled! How he tugged! And at last the bone came out, and two of Brer Wolf's big teeth with it.

"I'll skin you, Brer Rabbit, I'll skin you for this!" shouted Brer Wolf in a great rage. But Brer Rabbit was nowhere to be seen. Only a little song floated back on the wind to Brer Wolf, and made him dance with rage:

"*Hear him howl and hear him bellow,*
Old Brer Wolf is a silly old fellow!
He thought he'd grow three times as strong,
But old Brer Rabbit knows he's wrong!
Hear him howl and hear him bellow,
Isn't he a SILLY OLD FELLOW!"

Brer Rabbit and the Bellows

ONE DARK night, when nothing at all could be seen in the blackout, Brer Rabbit went early to bed. He opened his bedroom window before he jumped into bed, for he liked a bit of air at night.

And that's how it was that Brer Wolf got into Brer Rabbit's room ! He was prowling round with Brer Fox, who could see quite well in the dark—and they found Brer Rabbit's window open.

" Let's climb in and give Brer Rabbit a fright ! " said Brer Wolf, giggling. " We might even catch him asleep in bed, if we're quiet enough."

But they weren't quiet enough ! Brer Rabbit was awake and he heard their whispers. In a fright he leapt out of bed and ran to the best hiding-place he could think of—the chimney. He scrambled up a little way and then lay quiet.

Brer Wolf and Brer Fox didn't hear or see him. They padded softly to the bed and felt it.

" He's not here," whispered Brer Fox.

" But the bed's warm," said Brer Wolf. " Maybe he's gone to the kitchen for a drink of water ! We'll hide till he comes back."

And where did they choose to hide but just by the fireplace ! So poor Brer Rabbit couldn't get down and make a dive for the window. He was stuck there, and dared not move.

But by his paw was the handle of his bellows that he used when he wanted to blow his fire to make it burn well. Carefully Brer Rabbit pulled the bellows to him. He opened them—he pressed them together—and a big draught of air came from them and blew all over Brer Wolf !

"Don't, Brer Fox," said Brer Wolf angrily. "You make me cold."

"What do you mean, '*don't*'!" said Brer Fox, puzzled. "I didn't do anything."

"Yes, you did—you breathed down my neck," said Brer Wolf.

"I didn't," said Brer Fox crossly. Brer Rabbit blew some more air from his bellows and Brer Wolf shivered.

"There! You've done it again!" he said. "Don't! I hate you breathing on me."

"I'm not breathing anywhere near you," said Brer Fox in a huff.

Then Brer Rabbit puffed some air at Brer Fox, all over his head. Brer Fox twitched his ears and pushed Brer Wolf.

"Now you're breathing all over *me*," he said. "You make me very cold. Don't do it."

"I didn't," said Brer Wolf, "and if I did, well, it would just show you how horrid it is to be breathed over!"

"Go away from me," said Brer Fox, pushing Brer Wolf again. "Then you can't breathe down my neck."

Brer Rabbit puffed air in and out of the bellows and they made a noise like some great big person breathing hard. Brer Wolf and Brer Fox were startled.

"Do you hear that breathing noise, Brer Fox?" said Brer

Wolf. " There's some large person breathing quite close to us—I can hear him—it was he who breathed over us, I'm sure ! Who is it ? "

Brer Rabbit turned the bellows first on one, and then on the other of them. They began to shiver and shake.

" Who—who—who is it ? " said Brer Wolf in a trembling voice. " We can't see you."

" I'm Sniggle-Snaggle," said Brer Rabbit in a very deep voice from the chimney. " I've eaten Brer Rabbit all up—and I'm up the chimney waiting to come down and eat *you* up too, Brer Wolf and Brer Fox ! Urr-rrr-rrr-rrr ! "

Brer Wolf gave a howl of fright and tried to rush for the window. He fell over Brer Fox and trod on him. Brer Fox bit Brer Wolf's foot and made him howl again. Then, with Brer Rabbit jumping round them both in the darkness, puffing air down their necks, the two frightened animals leapt out of the window and made for the forest as fast as ever they could.

Brer Rabbit laughed and shut the window. He patted his bellows. " Thanks, Sniggle-Snaggle," he said to them. " You breathed well ! Now I'll get a little sleep, I think."

He hopped into bed and fell asleep. In the morning he awoke and looked out of the window. He saw Brer Fox and Brer Wolf telling a crowd of creatures all about how the Sniggle-Snaggle had eaten Brer Rabbit. Old Brer Rabbit laughed till he cried !

He walked out of his front door and waved to everybody. " Heyo ! " he cried. " Don't you believe a word those two rascals say ! *I* ate the Sniggle-Snaggle—it didn't eat me, for here I am, alive and kicking ! How did you like me breathing down your necks last night, Brer Wolf and Brer Fox ? "

Well ! Brer Wolf and Brer Fox stared at Brer Rabbit with their eyes and mouths wide open ! And to this day they don't know that the Sniggle-Snaggle was only Brer Rabbit's old pair of bellows !

Brer Rabbit's Bag

Now one day when Brer Rabbit was going home from market with his bag full of fish, lettuces, carrots, and meat, he met Brer Fox. Brer Fox was waiting for him behind a tree, and he jumped at Brer Rabbit as soon as he saw him.

But Brer Rabbit jumped too—and he was behind a tree before Brer Fox could say "Got you!"

He had to drop his bag though—and Brer Fox picked it up. "What's in here, Brer Rabbit?" he asked.

"Meat, fish, lettuces, and carrots," said Brer Rabbit sadly.

"Well, I don't want them," said Brer Fox. "You can have them, if you come and get them."

He looked quite kind, standing there, holding out the bag. Brer Rabbit thought he would see if he could grab it. So up he ran, put out his paw—but before he could snatch the bag, Brer Fox snatched *him*! And there was old Brer Rabbit, caught in Brer Fox's paw, and shaken like a rat.

"Ha! Now you're properly caught!" said Brer Fox. "And you'll just come along with me!"

So he dragged poor Brer Rabbit along with him, and his bag too, till he came to Brer Wolf's house. He went inside, shut the door, and showed Brer Wolf what he had caught.

"So you've got him at last!" said Brer Wolf, pleased. "Good! Put him in that cupboard, Brer Fox, for a minute, while we get the pot a-boiling. He's so smart I believe he'd get away if we didn't lock him up!"

So Brer Rabbit was put into a cupboard, where Brer Wolf kept his brooms and pots and pans and dishes. Bang! The

door was shut and locked. Brer Rabbit sat up and shivered. This was very bad. How in the world could he get away from that cupboard before Brer Fox came back?

It was no use hiding in any of the pots and pans. He would be found. And then an idea came into old Brer Rabbit's furry head.

He took all the goods out of his bag. He put the meat into a dish on the top shelf. He put the fish into another pot. He put the lettuces and carrots into a big pan on the top shelf too. He made a great noise doing it, and Brer Fox and Brer Wolf laughed.

"It's no good you rattling the pots and pans!" cried Brer Wolf. "You're in there and you can't get out, Brer Rabbit!"

What did Brer Rabbit do after he had hidden his goods, but get into the bag himself and shut it—snap! There he lay, as quiet as a mouse, waiting for the door to open.

When the pot was boiling on the fire, Brer Wolf went to the door of the cupboard. He opened it very carefully, in case Brer Rabbit should rush out. But no Brer Rabbit came. He opened the door wide—where *was* Brer Rabbit?

"Hie, Brer Fox! Where's Brer Rabbit?" said Brer Wolf, peering along the shelves.

Brer Fox came up and looked. He saw the bag at the bottom of the cupboard and he threw it out into the kitchen, thinking that maybe Brer Rabbit might be hiding behind it. But no Brer Rabbit was there !

Then those two began a wild hunt for old Brer Rabbit. They hunted on every shelf—but there was no Brer Rabbit to be seen!

If only they had looked behind them they would have seen Brer Rabbit all right. He opened the bag—snap ! He put out his long-eared head. He leapt out, ran to the door, opened it and disappeared under a bush. The door banged shut.

Brer Wolf and Brer Fox looked round at once. They saw the open, empty bag—and they knew at once what had happened.

" He threw out his goods, and got into the bag himself ! " groaned Brer Wolf. " Come on—after him ! "

They rushed out of the house, up the path, and through the gate. " He's gone that way, to the woods, I guess ! " cried Brer Fox—and off they went to the wood. As soon as they had gone out of sight, Brer Rabbit hopped out from the bush, went into Brer Wolf's house, collected all his goods from the cupboard, slipped them once more into his bag, and, whistling merrily, skipped out of the house and away to the fields, where he knew of a good safe burrow that ran nearby his house.

And didn't he laugh loudly whenever Brer Fox and Brer Wolf came by ! They went about looking as cross as two sticks for a whole month afterwards !

Brer Rabbit Ties Up Mr. Lion

ONE TIME Brer Rabbit was away in the middle of the woods when the wind began to blow. It blew so hard for a few minutes that Brer Rabbit thought maybe he'd better get out of the woods in case the wind blew a tree on top of him.

So he went off at a run, and my, when Brer Rabbit ran you could hardly see him go by, he went so fast! And whilst he was going along, full-tilt, he ran right into old Mr. Lion. Mr. Lion was astonished.

"Heyo, Brer Rabbit!" he said. "What's your hurry?"

"Run, Mr. Lion, run!" panted Brer Rabbit. "There's a big gale of wind coming! You'd better run!"

This made Mr. Lion sort of feel scared.

"I'm too heavy to run fast, Brer Rabbit. What shall I do?" he said.

"Lie down, then, Mr. Lion, lie down!" said Brer Rabbit. "Get close to the ground. Then you won't be blown over."

"Bless gracious, Brer Rabbit," said Mr. Lion. "If the wind's likely to blow away a little fellow like you whatever will it do to a big man like me? What shall I do?"

"Hug a tree, Mr. Lion, hug a tree!" shouted Brer Rabbit.

Mr. Lion lashed himself with his tail: "But suppose the gale of wind blows all day and night, Brer Rabbit?"

"Let me tie you to the tree, Mr. Lion," said Brer Rabbit, "let me tie you to the tree. Then you'll be quite safe!"

"Well, hurry then," said Mr. Lion. So Brer Rabbit fetched some string out of his pocket and tied Mr. Lion fast to a tree.

Then he sat down, Brer Rabbit did, and washed his face and his hands just like you see a cat doing. And he pulled down his ears and washed those too. Very soon Mr. Lion got tired of standing there tied to the tree, hugging the trunk, and he was surprised to see Brer Rabbit didn't go on running.

"Why don't you run away whilst you've got the chance?" he asked.

"Oh, I'm a-going to stay here and take care of you," said Brer Rabbit.

Soon Mr. Lion, who had been listening hard, spoke to Brer Rabbit again. "I can't hear any big wind," he said.

"I can't either," said Brer Rabbit, putting up his ears to listen.

"I can't hear so much as a leaf a-stirring," said Mr. Lion.

"I can't either," said Brer Rabbit.

Mr. Lion began to think hard. Brer Rabbit still sat there, he did, and went on washing his face and licking his paws.

"You'd better untie me now," said Mr. Lion at last.

"Oh no," said Brer Rabbit. "I'd be afraid to do that, Mr. Lion."

Then Mr. Lion got mighty mad, and he began to roar and bellow like twenty bulls. He bellowed so long and he bellowed so loud that presently all the creatures in the wood began to come along to see what was the matter.

As soon as Brer Rabbit saw them coming he began to talk mighty biggitty and strutted around like a peacock. And bless gracious, when the other creatures saw that Brer Rabbit had got Mr. Lion all tied up they stared and then ran off as quickly as they could.

"Brer Wolf, come and untie me!" yelled Mr. Lion.

"If Brer Wolf comes any nearer I'll tie him up too!" shouted Brer Rabbit.

"Brer Bear, come and untie me!" yelled Mr. Lion.

"Yes, you come, Brer Bear!" shouted Brer Rabbit. "And I'll take and tie you up with Mr. Lion too, so I will. You just come, Brer Bear!"

Brer Terrapin came up and stared a long time at Mr. Lion all tied up.

"What did you do that for, Brer Rabbit?" he said, with a grin.

"Oh, one day, a long time ago I went to the stream to get some water, and old Mr. Lion, he was there and he drove me away," said Brer Rabbit. "And ever since I've been waiting for a chance to catch him and tie him up. And here I've got him, and I guess he's mighty sorry he ever drove me away from that stream!"

"You untie me, Brer Rabbit, or I'll eat you, skin and all," bellowed Mr. Lion.

"You just stay there, Mr. Lion," said Brer Rabbit, "and you won't eat anybody! And what's more, if anyone dares to untie you I'll catch him and string him up so tightly he won't be able to move a claw! So just you hear that, Brer Possum and Brer Mink and Brer Fox! I can see you all a-peeping through the trees! Ha, you think Brer Rabbit's a mighty clever man, but you didn't know he was such a strong one too!"

And with that old Brer Rabbit went off home with Brer Terrapin—and didn't they laugh when they thought of Mr. Lion tied up there to the tree and nobody daring to untie him! Poor Mr. Lion—he had to chew the string in half himself—and then he went to look for Brer Rabbit. But Brer Rabbit was nowhere to be seen for a very long time!

Brer Rabbit and the Big Wind

ONCE WHEN Brer Rabbit was out walking, the wind got up and the trees began to sway. Brer Rabbit liked the wind. He held out his coat, let the wind fill it like a sail, and then off he went at top speed through the woods, shouting for joy.

Now Brer Bear was coming along, and suddenly Brer Rabbit bumped into him, and knocked all the breath out of his body. Brer Bear clutched at Brer Rabbit and held on tight.

"What's the matter now? What's all this? Why are you running so fast?" growled old Brer Bear angrily. "Knocking a fellow down like this—what's scaring you, Brer Rabbit?"

Brer Rabbit didn't like being held so tightly by Brer Bear. He wriggled and struggled, and he shouted in Brer Bear's ear.

"It's the Big Wind! My, I was running away from the Big Wind. And you'd better run too, I guess, Brer Bear, because if the Big Wind can blow a little fellow like me along so fast, what will it do to a big man like you? My, it will take you through the wood and drop you into the river as easy as can be!"

"Stars and moon!" said Brer Bear, frightened. "Where shall I hide?"

"Down a hole, Brer Bear, down a hole!" cried Brer Rabbit. "Quick, find a big one and get down it!"

Brer Bear let Brer Rabbit go and then lumbered off to a hole he knew. He squeezed down it, backwards way, and lay there with his head at the opening.

"The wind will blow your head off, Brer Bear!" cried Brer Rabbit, enjoying himself.

"Oh, what shall I do with it?" groaned Brer Bear.

"I'll put a big stone in front of the hole," said Brer Rabbit. "Then you'll be safe."

So he rolled a great stone in front of the hole, and then giggled to think how nicely he had trapped Brer Bear.

But he didn't grin long. No—he turned round, and there was old Brer Fox, ready to pounce on him! Brer Rabbit gave a squeal and stepped backwards.

"Now, you leave me alone!" he shouted to Brer Fox. "If you don't, I'll teach you such a lesson!"

"You speak boldly, Brer Rabbit," said Brer Fox, and he reached out his paw. "You won't speak quite so boldly in a minute."

"Now you listen to me, Brer Fox!" cried Brer Rabbit, squeezing into a bush as far as he could. "You just listen to me! If you so much as touch me I'll do the same to you as I've just done to Brer Bear!"

"And what's that?" asked Brer Fox, still grinning.

"I'll squash you down a hole and put a big stone in front of you," said Brer Rabbit.

Brer Fox laughed and laughed. "You show me where you've squashed Brer Bear into a hole, and I'll believe you," he said.

"Come along then," said Brer Rabbit, and he led Brer Fox round the bush to the hole where Brer Bear lay. Brer Bear was moaning and groaning because he felt very tightly squeezed in the hole—but he couldn't get out because of the big stone in front.

"There you are!" said Brer Rabbit. "Can't you hear him? Heyo, Brer Bear! Just tell old Brer Fox here that I rolled this stone in front of the hole. He won't believe me."

"Well, it's true enough," said Brer Bear with a groan, trying to get more comfortable. "Yes, Brer Rabbit put the stone there all right, Brer Fox. Oh, Brer Rabbit, let me out again now! I'm mighty uncomfortable."

Well, of course, Brer Fox didn't know that Brer Bear had gone into the hole because he was afraid of the Big Wind—

he just thought Brer Rabbit had squashed him into it himself, and had kept him there with the big stone.

So he looked mighty queer, and edged away from Brer Rabbit, feeling scared. Brer Rabbit grinned.

"Well," he said, "do you want to try and catch me now, Brer Fox? You're welcome! But I warn you, I'll put you into a hole too, and keep you there with a big stone in front till you say you're sorry. I think I'll put you there anyhow—yes, I will! Come here, Brer Fox, come here! I want to put you into a hole!"

But Brer Fox wasn't stopping. He fled away with a howl, wondering how it was that old Brer Rabbit seemed to be so strong all of a sudden.

And Brer Rabbit tore after him for all he was worth, though he didn't mean to catch him. No—not he! It was just a bit of fun chasing somebody who wanted to chase *him*—and HOW all the other creatures stared when they saw Brer Fox running away from old Brer Rabbit!

As for Brer Bear, he lay in his hole all day till Brer Wolf came along and let him out. And my, wasn't he angry with Brer Rabbit! You'd better keep out of Brer Bear's way for a week or two, Brer Rabbit, or you'll be sorry.